G

Home[...] ly, and
Carlos [...] down
the slope a ways, they stood up in a crouch and ran for their
horses. They mounted up quickly. Holmes saw them, and
snapped off a shot from his Henry rifle. He missed, but Bobtail saw him shoot and twisted his head to see what the sheriff had shot at. He saw Homer and Carlos riding away and
aimed his rifle.

"You sons of bitches," he shouted. He fired, his bullet
catching Carlos in the small of the back. Carlos flung his
arms up and fell backward over the horse's rump, turning a
flip and landing hard on his face and stomach.

Billy Pierce stood up and fired at Bobtail, catching him
between the shoulder blades. Bobtail fell forward at first,
then rocked back and sprawled out on the ground. Homer
was racing away as fast as he could go.

Slocum and the rest mounted up and rode toward the bodies. Holmes caught up with the dead man's horse and checked
the saddlebags.

"They're full of the stolen gold," he yelled. "Grab that
other one over there."

Slocum lit out after Homer.

Looking over his shoulder, Homer saw that he was being
chased. He had figured that Bobtail would keep them busy
long enough for him and Carlos to get safely away, but the
fool had turned and fired at his own buddies. Goddamn him
to hell. Homer lashed at his horse, but it was weighted down
with gold . . .

DON'T MISS THESE
ALL-ACTION WESTERN SERIES
FROM THE BERKLEY PUBLISHING GROUP

THE GUNSMITH by J. R. Roberts
Clint Adams was a legend among lawmen, outlaws, and ladies. They called him . . . the Gunsmith.

LONGARM by Tabor Evans
The popular long-running series about Deputy U.S. Marshal Custis Long—his life, his loves, his fight for justice.

SLOCUM by Jake Logan
Today's longest-running action Western. John Slocum rides a deadly trail of hot blood and cold steel.

BUSHWHACKERS by B. J. Lanagan
An action-packed series by the creators of Longarm! The rousing adventures of the most brutal gang of cutthroats ever assembled—Quantrill's Raiders.

DIAMONDBACK by Guy Brewer
Dex Yancey is Diamondback, a Southern gentleman turned con man when his brother cheats him out of the family fortune. Ladies love him. Gamblers hate him. But nobody pulls one over on Dex . . .

WILDGUN by Jack Hanson
The blazing adventures of mountain man Will Barlow—from the creators of Longarm!

TEXAS TRACKER by Tom Calhoun
J. T. Law: the most relentless—and dangerous—manhunter in all Texas. Where sheriffs and posses fail, he's the best man to bring in the most vicious outlaws—for a price.

JAKE LOGAN

SLOCUM

AND THE

KILLERS

J

JOVE BOOKS, NEW YORK

THE BERKLEY PUBLISHING GROUP
Published by the Penguin Group
Penguin Group (USA) Inc.
375 Hudson Street, New York, New York 10014, USA
Penguin Group (Canada), 90 Eglinton Avenue East, Suite 700, Toronto, Ontario M4P 2Y3, Canada
(a division of Pearson Penguin Canada Inc.)
Penguin Books Ltd., 80 Strand, London WC2R 0RL, England
Penguin Group Ireland, 25 St. Stephen's Green, Dublin 2, Ireland (a division of Penguin Books Ltd.)
Penguin Group (Australia), 250 Camberwell Road, Camberwell, Victoria 3124, Australia
(a division of Pearson Australia Group Pty. Ltd.)
Penguin Books India Pvt. Ltd., 11 Community Centre, Panchsheel Park, New Delhi—110 017, India
Penguin Group (NZ), 67 Apollo Drive, Rosedale, North Shore 0632, New Zealand
(a division of Pearson New Zealand Ltd.)
Penguin Books (South Africa) (Pty.) Ltd., 24 Sturdee Avenue, Rosebank, Johannesburg 2196,
South Africa

Penguin Books Ltd., Registered Offices: 80 Strand, London WC2R 0RL, England

This is a work of fiction. Names, characters, places, and incidents either are the product of the author's imagination or are used fictitiously, and any resemblance to actual persons, living or dead, business establishments, events, or locales is entirely coincidental.

SLOCUM AND THE KILLERS

A Jove Book / published by arrangement with the author

PRINTING HISTORY
Jove edition / April 2008

Copyright © 2008 by The Berkley Publishing Group.
Cover illustration by Sergio Giovine.

ISBN: 978-0-515-14448-2

JOVE®
Jove Books are published by The Berkley Publishing Group,
a division of Penguin Group (USA) Inc.,
375 Hudson Street, New York, New York 10014.
JOVE is a registered trademark of Penguin Group (USA) Inc.
The "J" design is a trademark belonging to Penguin Group (USA) Inc.

PRINTED IN THE UNITED STATES OF AMERICA

10 9 8 7 6 5 4 3 2 1

1

Slocum hired on with Trent Brady to help drive a herd of three hundred horses from Cheyenne, Wyoming, to Santa Fe, New Mexico. It promised to be a long and hard drive, but Slocum was tired of shooting wars. He knew Brady well and liked him, and he had done this kind of work before, plenty of times. He could stand it, and he could stand the drive. A week out from Cheyenne, he was convinced that he had made the right decision. He was enjoying the work. The days were long, but they were filled with plenty to keep him busy, with enough work to keep his mind off the kind of work he had been most recently involved in.

There were six hands altogether. Besides Trent Brady and Slocum, there was Billy Pierce, young and cocky, but a pretty good cowboy; Charlie Gourd, a half-breed Cherokee know-it-all; Old Jan, bearded and intellectual, but he knew horses; and Nebraska Ned, who had likely escaped a hangman's noose more than once. He was a good enough worker, though. The six of them handled the three hundred horses just fine.

The worst time of all for Slocum was when he tried to sleep at night, when he sat down around the campfire for a meal and a cup of coffee, any time when he was not working. Then he could think, or rather, he could not keep from

1

thinking. Then he recalled all the killings. Most of all, he thought about his last job.

Slocum had hired out on what he later discovered to be the wrong side of a range war. The man he had gone to work for, Laramie Johnson, was a no-good land-grabbing son of a bitch, but it had taken a while for Slocum to figure that out. Along with Reb Gillian, the hired gunslinger, he had already killed six of the opposition. Six good men trying to make an honest living for their families on small ranches. Johnson had told Slocum they were all part of a large band of rustlers, and Slocum had believed him. Like a damn fool. When Slocum figured out the truth, he had switched sides as fast as a locomotive switching tracks. He had killed Johnson and his main ringleaders, and the little men had won the war. Only Gillian had survived. They had won, but they had lost six good men, and Slocum was tormented.

Thoughts and memories of what he had done plagued Slocum unless he managed to keep himself busy. They surfaced in his mind to drive him crazy. They made him wish he had been a storekeeper or a banker or a farmer or even a barkeep. Sometimes, they made him wish he had died at birth. They intruded in his dreams. Nothing could drive the thoughts away but work. The busier the better. The more and harder the better. Slocum loved horses, and the work was good for him. He liked Trent Brady, and he was grateful to him for the job.

Slocum had worked all night and all day, and when night fell again, Brady had insisted that he get some sleep. Slocum and three others had bedded down while Brady and Nebraska Ned had ridden out to watch the herd. The bad dreams returned almost at once to Slocum's head, causing him to toss and turn in his sleep. Now and then he muttered or groaned. Old Jan sat up and stared at Slocum. In another moment, Gourd sat up.

"What's wrong with him?" Gourd asked.

"I don't know," said Jan. "Bad conscience, I'd guess."

"Humph," said Gourd. "Men like him ain't got a conscience."

Out on watch, Brady and Ned had separated, riding to opposite sides of the herd. Everything was quiet.

Over a hill not far away, three men sat around a small campfire drinking coffee.

"What's keeping Ham?" said one.

"Be patient, Hardy," said another. "He'll be back when he's found out something."

"Well, hell, I'm getting tired of just setting here on my ass. Hell, Sluice, I want to get this thing over with and behind us, so's we can get back to town and have a drink."

"Shut up, Hardy," said the third man. "Sluice knows what he's doing."

"Hardy," said Sluice, "I want that goddamned Brady. No one gets away with what he done to me. No one."

"Well, hell, Sluice," said Hardy, "all he done was to testify at your trial that he seen you kill that man. He told the truth was all."

"And they sentenced me to hang, didn't they?"

"Yeah, but we broke you out of jail."

"And now we're all fucking fugitives from justice, ain't we? It wouldn't have hurt that son of a bitch a goddamned bit to just've kept his damn mouth shut. Wouldn't have hurt him none at all. Well, now he's going to pay."

They heard the sound of an approaching horse, and all three men jumped to their feet and hauled out their six-shooters, moving a distance away from the fire. The rider came closer.

"It's Ham," said Hardy.

They holstered their weapons. Ham dismounted and walked to the fire, pouring himself a cup of coffee. "Just over the hill," he said, "Brady's by hisself. Well, there's another rider out with him, but he's on the other side of the herd."

"Just two of them out there?" Sluice said.

"That's all."

"Come on," Sluice said. "Let's get going."

"Can't I finish my coffee?" Ham asked.

Sluice kicked the cup from Ham's hand. "I said now," he yelled.

"Ow. You hurt my fingers."

"Shut up and get mounted."

Ham picked up his cup from the ground and stood up. He looked longingly into the cup and saw about a slurp left there. He turned it down and dropped the cup. He walked back to his horse and mounted up again.

"You'd think a man could at least drink a cup of coffee," he muttered. "Get his fingers kicked. Shit."

When all four men were mounted, Sluice said, "Lead the way, Ham."

Trent Brady rode slowly and sang softly. He had a couple of hours left on his watch, but he was content with the chore. Like Slocum, he loved horses, and he enjoyed this quiet time with them. He was in no hurry to be relieved. He had a fine bunch of animals, and he was looking forward to a hell of a good payday at the end of the drive.

High up on a nearby hill, Sluice and his boys sat looking down on the horse herd and the two riders. Sluice pulled out his revolver and checked it one last time. He was nervous. He was anxious.

"Hey, Sluice," said Hardy, "if we was to ride about halfway down this hill, I could pick off both of them bastards with my Henry rifle."

"I know you could," Sluice answered, "but I don't want you to do that. I want to look that fart Brady right in the face. I want him to know how come he's going to die. I want him to know who it is fixing to kill him."

"What about the other one?" Hardy asked.

"I don't give a shit about him," Sluice said. "Go ahead and take your position, but don't do nothing till I've got Brady."

"I got you, Sluice."

"All right, the rest of you, let's get going."

They all started riding down the hill. About halfway down the hill, Hardy pulled up beside a boulder and dismounted, pulling his Henry rifle out of the saddle boot.

"Hardy," Sluice snapped, "remember what I said."

"Don't worry, Sluice," Hardy answered. "I'll wait for you."

Sluice led the others on down the hill. They moved slowly so as not to cause an alarm, not to spook the horse herd. Trent Brady was clear over on the other side. When Sluice and his boys had reached the bottom of the hill undetected, they moved cautiously to the rear of the herd and around to the other side. The sky was clear. There was no wind. As the gang moved closer, each man with his revolver in his hand, they could hear Brady singing softly.

They moved closer. The sound of horses' hooves, of course, was not alarming, but when Brady heard the creaking of saddle leather, he spun his own mount around and found himself facing three men with drawn six-guns, all pointed directly at him. His hand automatically went for his own sidearm, but Ham fired a shot that broke his right arm. He dropped the gun.

"Ah," he groaned. "What the hell—"

"Trent Brady, you dog-shit son of a bitch," said Sluice, "you remember me?"

"Sluice Godfrey," said Brady. "Yeah. I know you."

"Good," Sluice said. "I mean to kill you for what you done to me."

Brady thought about Slocum and the others sleeping not far away. He thought about Nebraska Ned across the way on the opposite side of the herd. He knew that none of them could get to him in time. He felt the numbness in his right arm, and he could feel the blood flowing freely down to his hand and dripping off and falling to the ground. He knew that it was over. His time had come.

"You did it all to yourself, you cheap, cowardly killer," he said.

"Goddamn you to hell," said Sluice, and he fired a bullet that hit Brady in the chest.

Across the way and up the hill, Hardy heard the shots. So did Ned down at the bottom of the hill. Ned looked around. He turned his horse to ride around the herd. Hardy put his rifle to his shoulder, took careful aim, and fired. Ned toppled from the saddle. Hardy mounted his horse and started down the hill to make sure of his shot and to join the others. The horse herd was stamping and milling about.

Trent Brady was still sitting in the saddle, sagging, bleeding badly.

"Finish him, Sluice," said Ham.

"Shut up," Sluice said. "I'm enjoying this."

Jigs, the fourth outlaw, said, "Sluice, his hands'll be coming."

"All right," said Sluice, "all right," and he fired another shot into Brady's chest. Brady slipped slowly from the saddle and fell hard to the ground. He did not move.

Back at the camp, Slocum and the others came to their feet fast at the sounds of the shots. They pulled on their boots, strapped on their gun belts, and hurried to saddle their horses. Slocum was thinking the whole time, "We'll be too late." Nevertheless, he mounted his big Appaloosa as fast as he could and headed for the herd. He was followed quickly by the others.

Sluice and his two boys headed back the way they had come. They fired their guns all the way, causing the horse herd to stampede. On the far side of the herd, Hardy had been riding toward the fallen Ned to make sure he was dead. He had come close to where Ned had fallen when the herd began to run. He looked ahead and saw Sluice and the others riding hard toward him. He turned and rode toward them. As Sluice and the others raced up the hill, they continued firing, driving the horse herd on its way.

Halfway up the hill, Ham's horse slipped on the steep ground and took a hard tumble, landing hard on its side and on Ham's leg. Ham heard and felt the leg snap. He screamed in pain. The other three continued racing ahead.

"Sluice," Ham screamed. "I'm down. Goddamn it. I'm down."

"Ham's down," said Hardy.

"Fuck him," said Sluice. "Keep riding."

"Come back," screamed Ham, watching the three horses and riders growing smaller in his vision. "I'm hurt here. Come back. You shit fucks. You sons of bitches. You goat assholes. Help me here. Oh, hell. Oh, damn it."

Slocum was first on the scene. He saw the end of the horse herd as it was disappearing up ahead. He rode on, and then he saw Trent Brady lying on the ground. Brady's horse was nowhere in sight. Likely, it had run with the herd. It would probably become a wild horse burdened by a saddle on its back. Slocum raced over to where Brady lay and jumped from the saddle, running to Brady's side and kneeling. He picked up Brady's head and cradled it in his arms.

"Trent," he said. "Trent."

"Sloo—" said Brady. "Sloo—" His head dropped, and he said no more.

"Damn," said Slocum. "Damn it."

The other riders came up behind Slocum.

Billy Pierce dismounted. "Is he—"

"Dead," said Slocum.

"Let's look for Ned," Charlie Gourd said.

Billy, Charlie, and Old Jan began riding around and looking. Before long, Old Jan yelled, "Over here, boys."

They rode to where Old Jan was waiting beside the body of Nebraska Ned. When they hauled up on their reins, Old Jan shook his head. "He's gone, too," he said. They picked up the body and rode back to where Slocum still sat holding Trent Brady. They all dismounted.

"Ned's been killed, too," Charlie said.

Slowly, Slocum laid down the lifeless head. Slowly, he stood up. He took a deep breath. "We'd best bury them," he said.

"Right now?" said Charlie. "Here?"

"You got a better idea?" Slocum asked.

"I'll ride back to camp and fetch the shovels," said Charlie. He mounted up and headed back for the camp.

"We could round up that herd in the morning," said Billy Pierce.

"You do what you want to do," Slocum said.

"You mean you ain't going after the herd?" asked Billy.

"It ain't mine," said Slocum. "It was Trent's."

"Well, what're you going to do, Slocum?" Old Jan asked.

"I'm going after the killers," Slocum said, "and I mean to get them."

"They're likely horse thieves," said Old Jan.

"I don't think so," Slocum said, "but come daylight, we'll check the signs. Trent was still alive when I found him. Barely. He said something that sounded like 'sloo.' Said it twice. 'Sloo, sloo.' That mean anything to any of you?"

"Sloo?" said Billy. "I don't think so."

"Wait a minute," said Old Jan. "There was a murder trial a while back. Trent was a witness. The only eyewitness. He testified at the trial and got the killer sentenced to hang. Man's name was Sluice Godfrey."

"Sluice," said Slocum. "Could be."

Charlie came riding back with shovels, and he and Billy started digging. The whinny of a horse sounded from somewhere across the way.

"You hear that?" said Old Jan.

"Yeah," said Slocum.

"It sounded to me like a hurt horse," said Old Jan.

Slocum moved to his Appaloosa and swung into the saddle. "Let's find it," he said.

They rolled across the flat to the base of the hill. They heard it again. They sat still, looking around. The horse neighed yet again. It sounded like a call for help.

"Up the hill," said Old Jan. "There."

They rode up to the hurt horse and found a man pinned underneath it. The man saw the two riders.

"Help me," he whined.

"Your buddies ride off and leave you?" Slocum asked.

"Yeah. The dirty shits," said Ham.

"Who are they?" Slocum demanded.

"Get this horse off me," said Ham. "I'm hurt. I think my leg's broke."

"If you don't tell me your name," said Slocum, "and the names of your pards, you'll just stay there. I will put your horse out of its misery, though."

Slocum pulled out his Colt and fired, and the hurt horse felt no more pain. Ham flinched and shivered. He felt the weight of the animal, already heavy, now a deadweight, sink down even heavier on his wretched leg.

"Mister, please," he said.

"Tell me their names," Slocum said.

"All right. All right," said Ham. "It was Sluice. Sluice and Hardy and Jigs. They call me Ham. Now help me out of here. Please."

"I'll help you just like I helped your horse," Slocum said.

"What?" said Ham. "No. No."

Slocum shot him in the head.

2

"Goddamn, Slocum," said Old Jan. "You just murdered the son of a bitch."

"It was better than he deserved," Slocum said. "He was with them that killed Trent."

"Yeah," said Old Jan. "Well, I don't know what else we can do here tonight. Can't follow tracks or nothing till morning light."

"I guess you're right," Slocum agreed. "Let's go back to our camp."

They rode down the hill and back across the way to where Billy and Charlie had finished digging the holes for the two graves.

"I heard a couple of shots," said Billy.

"There was one they left behind under a hurt horse," said Old Jan. "He was pinned under the horse and hurt, too. Slocum put them both out of their misery."

Charlie jabbed his shovel down into the fresh-dug pile of dirt. "Let's get this over with," he said.

They lowered the bodies into the graves. Slocum stood close to the one in which they lowered Trent Brady. He took the hat off his head. "I promise you, pard," he said. "I'll get the dirty bastards. I'll kill every one of them. I promise you."

They finished the unpleasant chore and rode back to camp. The three men were soon asleep, but Slocum put more coffee on the fire. He lit a cigar and waited for the coffee to boil. He sat up all night. He did not know this Sluice, would not know him when he saw him, but he was determined to find him as well as the rest of the men who had ridden with him. That worthless shit Ham had said their names were Hardy and Jigs. He would find them, and he would kill them. He was anxious for the first light of the new day.

He spent the night smoking and drinking coffee and thinking about Trent Brady. He could not help thinking about Sluice and Hardy and Jigs. He would find them somehow, somewhere. Interestingly enough, the thoughts that had been tormenting his nights had at last been pushed aside by these new ones. He made sure that his Colt and his Winchester were fully loaded and ready for action. He was damn sure ready for it himself.

When the sun at last peeked over the far horizon, Slocum started saddling his stallion. He didn't bother waking up the others. He did not care what they did. He had his business to take care of. Let them sleep. Let them go their own ways. He did not give a damn about what they did. He mounted up and rode toward the graves. When he got there, he studied the hoofprints. It looked to Slocum like there had been three riders where Trent was killed.

He studied the tracks long and hard. It looked to Slocum like the three bastards had ridden up behind Trent, killed him, and turned to retrace their tracks. He followed them back around to where the herd had been, across the way and up the hill to where Ham was pinned underneath his horse. He took note that something had been feasting on the two bodies. He studied some more. Apparently, a fourth outlaw had not gone with the other three to kill Trent. He had stopped near where Ham had later died. From a boulder nearby, he had killed Ned with his rifle. Then the others had rejoined him, and as they were racing away, Ham's horse had fallen. The other three had simply kept going up the hill. Without looking back, without a thought to his own three companions, Slocum continued following the tracks.

"Sluice," said Hardy. "We been riding the whole fucking night. These horses are damn near fagged out."

"We'll trade them in for some fresh ones here pretty soon," Sluice said. "There's a little ranch just a couple of miles ahead."

"You think the rancher will trade with us?" Jigs asked.

Sluice gave Jigs a look, as if he thought that Jigs was an idiot. Hardy laughed.

"I ain't never met a man who wouldn't trade horses with Sluice," he said, "if Sluice just asks him right."

"Oh," said Jigs. "Yeah. I get it now." He laughed as well, and Sluice joined in the laughter.

"I reckon they'll feed us some breakfast, too," Sluice said.

"If we ask them real nice!" said Hardy.

They all broke into fresh laughter.

They rode on a few more miles and then spotted the ranch. It was a small family place. A tiny house, no bunkhouse, a corral a few feet away from the house. Smoke rose from the chimney. A man was in the corral. The three killers rode down to the house and over to the corral. The man looked up when they approached.

"Howdy, boys," he said.

"Howdy, pardner," Sluice said. "We're riding good horses, but they're tired right now. Wonder if you might trade with us?"

"Sorry," the man said. "I got nothing I want to trade off. You're welcome to rest them up here for a spell, though."

"That's mighty kind of you," Sluice said. "I don't suppose you could spare some breakfast. We could pay you."

"I reckon so," the man said. "Climb down out of your saddles and come with me."

He led the way into the house, where his wife was busy fixing breakfast. A boy, about seven or eight years old, was in the house as well. The man introduced his wife and son. The wife poured the visitors cups of coffee.

"Y'all run this whole place just by yourselfs?" Sluice asked. "No hands?"

"It's a small place," said the rancher. "A family operation. Just us."

"Well, I'll be," said Sluice.

The woman put breakfast out on the table, and they all ate voraciously. Sluice and his boys ate their fill and asked for more coffee. They finished their coffee and stood up as if to leave. Then Sluice, with no warning, pulled out his six-gun and shot the boy. Taking their cue from Sluice, Hardy jerked his gun and shot the woman, and Jigs hauled out his and killed the man.

"Rummage around, boys," said Sluice. "Take any food and anything else you think we can use."

They packed away some food, a couple of boxes of bullets, and a few dollars and change. Then Sluice had them set fire to the house. They went out to the corral and picked out three good-looking horses, switched their saddles, mounted up, and rode on out.

Slocum followed the prints of the three horses all morning and into the afternoon, when he came across the smoldering ashes of a recent fire. The hoofprints he was following went down to the corral, which stood a short distance from the ashes. He rode down there and dismounted. Walking around and studying the tracks, he figured out that the men had changed horses there. He saw the prints of the three new horses leading away from the site. He started to mount up and continue following them, but he decided instead to investigate the fire. What he found horrified him. Slocum had seen much. He had taken part in much violence himself. But when he found the remains of the little family, he renewed his vow of vengeance against Sluice and Hardy and Jigs. He decided that he needed to get them as quickly as possible. The longer they rode free, the more victims they would have. They had to die, and soon.

Slocum followed the tracks of the new horses away from the ruined ranch. He rode the rest of that day. When night fell, he could ride no more. He had been awake for most of two days and two nights and needed some sleep. He located a good campsite and settled in for the night—a short night, he told himself. He built a small fire, had a quick meal, and made some coffee. Waiting for his coffee to boil, he smoked a cigar. His thoughts were all on the three inhuman monsters he was tracking.

When his coffee was ready, he poured himself a cup. He had just taken a first sip when he heard the sounds of approaching horses. Setting down his coffee, he pulled out his Colt and moved away from the fire. He listened as the horses came closer in the darkness. He pulled back the hammer on the Colt and held it ready. Then three riders came into view in the light of the campfire.

"Slocum?" said Old Jan. "You here?"

Slocum eased the hammer back down on the Colt and stepped out into view.

"Coffee's on," he said.

Old Jan, Charlie Gourd, and Billy Pierce all swung down out of their saddles. They started taking care of their horses for the night.

"What brings you three around here?" Slocum asked.

"What brings us around?" said Old Jan. "Hell, we want those bastards as much as you do."

"You couldn't wait on us, could you?" said Gourd. "Couldn't wake us up before you took off?"

"Hell," said Slocum. "You were sleeping like a bunch of babies. I didn't have the heart to wake you up."

"Let me at that coffee," said Billy.

"Help yourself," Slocum said.

"You see what those sons of bitches done back down the trail?" said Gourd.

"I saw it," said Slocum.

"We've got to stop them," said Old Jan.

"I mean to," Slocum said.

"We're all agreed on that," Gourd said.

"How far ahead of us do you reckon they are?" Pierce asked.

"A day's ride," Slocum answered.

"We'll have to ride hard to catch up with them," said Billy.

"They'll slow down and stop before much longer," said Gourd. "They'll wear their horses out otherwise."

"That won't slow them," Slocum said. "They'll just steal more."

"And kill more in the doing of it," Old Jan added.

"They'll kill anyone," said Gourd. "They proved that back there at that ranch."

A northbound stagecoach was bouncing along the road to Cheyenne loaded up with passengers, a driver, and a shotgun rider on top. Inside the coach were two ladies, one about thirty years old, the other maybe fifty, and three men, a cowboy, a traveling salesman, and a stern-faced old preacher. As the coach rounded a curve in the road, going uphill, it suddenly came upon three men standing across the road with guns in their hands. The shotgun rider instinctively raised his weapon, only to be shot dead by Hardy. As he crumpled in the seat, Sluice and Jigs both blasted the driver from the box and watched him fall to the ground.

"Grab them horses, Jigs," ordered Sluice as he ran to one side of the coach, Hardy to the other. They grabbed the doors and jerked them open. The passengers all had horrified looks on their faces.

"What have you done?" asked the preacher. "Have you killed them?"

"Something damn sure did," said Sluice. "All of you get out on this side."

"Don't hurt us," said the older woman.

"Shut up, lady," said Sluice. "Hardy, climb up there and check the boot."

Hardy went up on top and found a box. He heaved it out and threw it to the ground. Then he tossed all the bags and boxes down from the roof.

"Check the rear," said Sluice. Hardy climbed back down

and went around to the back. He pulled out all the luggage and threw it to the ground.

"All right, Jigs," said Sluice. "You can turn them horses loose."

Jigs turned loose the lead horse he had been holding. It did not run, so he slapped it on the rump. The horses took off dragging the empty stage behind them.

"Here," said the preacher.

"Shut up," said Sluice.

"But how will we get to town?" said the older woman.

"If I was you," said Sluice, "that'd be the last of my worries. Now all of you empty out your pockets."

"This is outrageous," said the preacher. "You'll all hang, and your souls will go to hell."

"Shut up, you fucking Bible-thumper," said Sluice. He cocked his revolver and pointed it close to the preacher's face. "Empty your goddamned pockets."

Moving along the road, Slocum and the others came across the abandoned stagecoach.

"Oh, my God," said Gourd. "Are you thinking what I'm thinking?"

They rode on up to the stage. Slocum climbed up top and found the body of the shotgun rider crumpled up below the seat. Old Jan opened a door and looked inside.

"No one here," he said.

"One dead man on top," said Slocum, climbing back down. "Cut those horses loose and let's move along."

Billy Pierce and Charlie Gourd had the horses freed in record time. They remounted their horses and hurried along the road. In a few miles, they found the bodies and the scattered luggage. Each of the passengers and the driver had been shot to death. But there was one addition. The younger of the two women was somewhat separated from the others, and it appeared that she had been ravished before she had been shot to death. Slocum and his partners checked the pockets of the dead. They had all been emptied. The cash box had been emptied. Each piece of luggage had been searched. Anything the outlaws did not want had been scattered along the road. There were no guns anywhere. The killers had taken them as well.

"More reasons for killing those bastards," said Pierce.

"We don't need more reasons," said Gourd. "We've got plenty already."

"I think we should bury these poor people," said Old Jan.

Slocum mounted his Appaloosa.

"What are you doing, Slocum?" said Gourd. "Where you going?"

"After them."

"What about burying these folks?"

"You three go ahead," said Slocum, and he turned his horse and kicked it in the sides, hurrying away from the scene of the slaughter.

"Well, how about that?" said Gourd.

"I wouldn't have thought he'd have rode off and left us with this chore," said Billy Pierce.

"Likely, he figures he's got more important things to deal with," said Old Jan. "These folks here are beyond help. Those we're after sure need to be stopped."

"Maybe," said Gourd, "but still, he could've stuck around till the burying was done."

"No, Charlie," said Old Jan. "Slocum couldn't have. He had to go. Now, let's get to digging some graves."

Slocum rode with a fury. If anything, he was feeling the sense of urgency more than ever. Sluice and his two wild animals had to be stopped and soon. Slocum had never before wanted so badly to kill someone. And he wanted to do it in a hurry. He slowed down now and then only to make sure he was still following the right tracks. They went straight ahead as if the killers had no idea or no concern that they might be followed. He hoped they stayed that way. With so much confidence, they might stop somewhere soon to relax. That would be all he needed. He would catch them and kill them.

Soon, he had to slow the Appaloosa. He hated to slow down, but he knew the horse could not stand too much running at top speed. It could take more than most, but even it had its limitations. He would walk it for a while, then he would run again. The tracks were still plain. The killers did not appear to be in a hurry.

3

Jigs rode a little ahead of his two compadres, and when he topped a rise he saw a sight he wasn't expecting. He turned and rode fast back to Sluice and Hardy. "Hey, guess what's just over that hill."

"I ain't in the mood for guessing games," Sluice said. "What is it?"

"That horse herd we run off."

"Hey," said Hardy, "we could take them and sell them for a pretty penny."

"Don't be stupid," said Sluice. "We don't know how many cowpokes ole Brady had with him. They might be trailing that herd."

"Besides," said Jigs, "that sounds like too much work."

"Yeah," said Sluice, "but they can help us out."

"What are you talking about, Sluice?" said Hardy. "How can they help us out?"

"Someone might be on our trail. We can ride down there amongst them horses and lose our tracks."

"Goddamn," said Jigs. "You're right."

"Come on," said Sluice. "Let's go."

They rode up over the hill and down into the valley below. Soon, they were in the midst of the milling horse herd.

As soon as Sluice and his boys moved in, the herd became uneasy and started to move.

"Keep with them," Sluice yelled.

Moving into the herd, Jigs noticed something. "Looky there," he said. The other two saw the horse with a saddle running with the others. Sluice laughed out loud.

"That must be old Brady's horse," he said.

"He'll get tired pretty soon running with this bunch with a saddle on his back," said Hardy.

They rode with the herd for a couple of miles before they moved out in their own direction. They rode back up over the hill and down onto the trail again, but this time they kept off to the side of the road, so they would leave no tracks. Then they continued moving in a southwesterly direction.

"That ought to cover our tracks," Sluice said.

"If anyone was following us," said Hardy, "he'll lose us for sure now."

"That's right," Sluice said, "but be sure you don't leave any tracks on the road here."

"Say, Sluice," said Hardy, "ain't there a town up ahead?"

"Yeah," said Sluice. "North Fork. It ain't far."

"I could sure use a drink," said Jigs.

"And a woman," said Hardy.

"Or a few women," Jigs said.

"Hell," said Sluice, "a whole damn herd of women."

The three of them burst into raucous laughter.

Following Slocum's trail, Gourd, Pierce, and Old Jan were riding hard. They could see Slocum's tracks and the tracks of the three riders he was following. It was easy trailing.

"Goddamn Slocum," said Gourd. "He can't ever wait for no one, can he?"

"It's all right," said Old Jan. "His tracks are easy enough to follow. He knows we're back here behind him."

"But what's he going to do if he catches up with them before we catch up with him?" asked Billy Pierce.

"He won't wait," said Old Jan. "He'll try to kill them. All three of them."

"Goddamn fool," said Gourd.

Slocum followed the tracks of his prey to the horse herd. There he lost them. He searched for some time, but to no avail. He did throw a rope over Trent Brady's horse and unsaddle it before he let it go again. At last, he decided to go back to the main trail. He couldn't decide what else to do. He figured that once the three men had hidden their tracks in those of the herd, they might move back to the road. There did not seem to be any other place they could go that made any sense. He knew that the town of North Fork was not far ahead. He figured he would find them there.

Sluice dismounted at the rail in front of the Watering Hole Saloon in North Fork. Jigs and Hardy started to do the same, but Sluice stopped them. "You two tie your horses down the street," he said. "Not together, neither. And when you come inside, keep away from me."

"How come?" asked Jigs.

"Just do it, asshole," Sluice said.

Jigs shrugged and rode down the street, followed by Hardy. Sluice tied his horse and went inside. He walked straight to the bar and pounded on it. The bartender came over to him.

"What'll it be, stranger?"

"Whiskey," said Sluice. "A bottle."

The barkeep produced a bottle, and Sluice paid for it with some of the money he had gotten from the stagecoach. He poured himself a drink and downed it. Then he turned to look around the room. He decided to stay at the bar.

Outside on the wooden sidewalk, Jigs and Hardy walked together toward the saloon.

"What's up with Sluice?" said Jigs.

"Damned if I know," said Hardy.

"Tell us to tie up down the street and stay away from him in the saloon. What the fuck is he up to?"

"Hell," said Hardy, "just go along with him. That's all."

They reached the saloon and walked in. They spotted Sluice standing at the bar and looked at him. He looked back and gave them a slight nod of the head. They walked to the bar to stand some distance away from Sluice. The barkeep approached them.

"A bottle and two glasses," said Hardy.

"Whiskey?" asked the barkeep.

"What else?" said Hardy.

The barkeep brought the order, and Hardy paid for it, the same way Sluice had paid for his. He looked around, spotted a table, and nodded to it. He and Jigs went to the table, pulled out chairs, and sat down. Hardy poured the glasses full, and they both drank. A couple of saloon girls were milling around, and Jigs had his eyes on them.

"Look at that one," he said. "I bet she'd be hot."

"Hell, you had some not that long ago," Hardy said.

"That was then. This is now."

One of the gals came slithering up to their table. She had her eye on the bottle in front of the two men. "Buy a girl a drink?" she asked.

"Sit down, sweet tits," said Jigs.

The gal giggled and sat down next to Jigs. She waved at the barkeep for a glass, and he brought one over. Hardy poured her a drink.

"What's your name?" he said.

"They call me Bitsy," she said. "What's yours?"

"I'm Jigs."

"I'm Hardy."

Over at the bar, Sluice heard the conversation, and he called himself six kinds of a fool for not having told those two to keep their names to themselves. At least, no one knew that he was with them. He watched them in the mirror behind the bar. He saw them as the two of them got up from the table with the gal, took their bottle and three glasses with them, and headed for the stairway. He cursed them silently as they mounted the stairs. When they disappeared at the top of the stairway, he poured himself another drink.

Slocum rode into North Fork looking for three horses. He expected to find them in front of the saloon, but he did not. He tied his Appaloosa at the rail and went inside. He looked around the room, but saw no one who aroused his curiosity. He didn't see three men together anywhere. He stepped up to the bar noticing only one other man there. The bartender approached him.

"What'll it be?" he asked.

"I'm looking for three men who rode through here together," Slocum said.

"I ain't seen three men together," said the barkeep. "I—"

Sluice interrupted. "I couldn't help but overhear you, stranger," he said. "I seen three riders."

"Where'd they go?" Slocum asked.

"These men friends of yours?"

"Not hardly."

"You're after them then," said Sluice.

"I mean to kill them," said Slocum.

"Well, I don't know if it's the right men or not," Sluice said, "but three rough-looking rannies rode through town about an hour ago. Rode straight through. Seemed to be in a hurry. Maybe on account of you, huh?"

"Could be," said Slocum. "They headed south?"

"That's right."

"Thanks," Slocum said. He turned and walked back out the door. Sluice poured himself another drink.

Upstairs, Hardy was lying naked on the bed with a drink in his hand. Bitsy was equally unclothed and on her hands and knees between his legs slurping at his member. Behind her, Jigs was on his knees, his rod pumping in and out of her twat. Slap, slap, slap, he banged against her rump. "Yahoo," Jigs shouted. "Ride 'em. Ride 'em."

All of a sudden, Hardy opened his eyes wide, and his jaw dropped. "Oh. Oh. Oh," he said as his rod let loose salvo after salvo into Bitsy's mouth. His fingers relaxed, and he dropped the glass, spilling whiskey all over his hairy belly. When he at last stopped coming, Bitsy let the drooping tool slip out of her mouth, and she inched forward, licking whiskey off his belly. As she did so, she pulled loose of Jigs's cock. It popped from her cunt and slapped up against his belly.

"Goddamn," he said. "I ain't done."

Bitsy flopped over onto her back and said, "Well, come on, cowboy. Shove it back in." Jigs scrambled between her legs and began poking furiously, but he couldn't find the hole. Bitsy reached down with both hands and guided it in. "That's good," she said. "Oh, yeah."

Hardy sat up on the edge of the bed and poured himself another drink. Just then the door burst open, and Sluice stepped in.

"Get your damn clothes on," he said. "You got a job to do."

"What the hell?" said Jigs, his rod suddenly going limp.

"Just get dressed and hurry up," said Sluice. He looked at Bitsy. "And you get out of here."

"I ain't been paid," she said.

"Pay her and get rid of her," Sluice said.

Hardy picked up his britches and dug out some cash. He handed some to Bitsy. She picked up her clothes and ran out of the room. Hardy was pulling on his britches.

"What's up, Sluice?" he asked.

"I was right," Sluice said. "Someone was following us. I sent him on a wild-goose chase out of town. He'll be looking ahead of hisself for us, so we can slip up on him from behind and kill him. Come on. Hurry it up."

Outside of town, Slocum rode the trail slowly looking for sign that three riders had gone ahead of him. He did not find any, but he had lost the tracks going into North Fork. These three must be skilled at covering their tracks, he thought. Well, hell, they would surface sooner or later. The trail was winding through the foothills of the mountains. There were boulders on each side. The trail had narrowed, and it moved up a rise. Slocum reached the top of the rise and started down again.

Back behind him, Hardy rode alone ahead of his two cronies. He topped the rise not long after Slocum, and he looked down and saw Slocum riding slowly and studying the trail. He turned his horse and hurried back down to where Sluice and Jigs were waiting. "He's right over the top of this hill," he said. "Down in the valley."

"Close enough to get a shot?" said Sluice.

"I can get him," said Hardy.

"Come on," said Sluice, and he kicked his horse in the sides. The three men rode fast to the top of the rise. They stopped there and looked down. Slocum was still in sight. The three dismounted, and Hardy took the rifle out of his saddle boot. He moved to the edge of the road and leaned on a boulder. He put the rifle to his shoulder and took careful aim. Slocum was riding along the edge of a drop-off. Hardy cocked his rifle, waited a couple of seconds, and fired.

Slocum felt the slug tear into his shoulder, and he toppled from his horse. He was very near the edge of the drop-off. He was aware of the danger he was in. Whoever had plugged him would likely come to see that the job was done. He looked over his shoulder down into the drop-off below. He thought that he could survive the fall. He rolled and went over, landing hard on a boulder. He looked up. He was in a position where he thought he could see if anyone looked over the edge, but they could not see him. He squirmed a little, moving himself in closer to the wall to be sure. He could still see up there. He waited.

"Come on," said Sluice. "Let's make sure of him."

He started riding down the hill with Jigs right beside him. Hardy mounted his horse and followed them. Slocum's Appaloosa saw them coming and ran farther on down the road. They stopped where the Appaloosa had been, dismounted, and walked to the edge of the drop-off. Leaning over, they looked down.

"I don't see no sign of him, Sluice," said Jigs.

"Me neither," said Hardy, "but he went over right here."

"That's a hard fall," said Sluice. "With your slug in him and that fall, he's done for all right. If one didn't kill him, the other one did. Or else he'll lay there where he landed and bleed to death. Even if he could crawl back up here, which I sure as hell doubt, his horse is gone. He's a dead man all right. Let's move along."

They mounted up and headed south along the road.

Down below, Slocum had seen their faces. One, he thought, was the same son of a bitch he had seen back in the saloon. The one who had told him that three men passed through town. And one of the other two had called him Sluice. Slocum cursed himself for having been suckered by the bastard. He'd had him right there in North Fork. Right in the saloon. He could have killed him then and there. Oh, well, now that he had seen him, he'd know him the next time. The next time he would kill him.

The next time. There might not be a next time. He had a hole in his shoulder, and it was bleeding badly. He was down on the side of a drop-off, and he did not feel like he could get himself back up to the road. Even if someone came along, they wouldn't see him where he was. He had made sure of that. He wondered if this would be his end. He wasn't afraid of that, but he damn sure regretted not getting Sluice and his pals. He groaned. The gunshot wound was beginning to hurt. The pain sent throbs through his body. And he hurt where he had banged his body into the rocks. He did not think anything was broken, but he wasn't sure. It did not seem to matter, though. He couldn't move. Then the world suddenly grew dim and then dark, and Slocum drifted into unconsciousness.

Back down the road, Old Jan, Billy Pierce, and Charlie Gourd were just riding into North Fork.

4

Gourd, Pierce, and Old Jan tied their horses in front of the Watering Hole and went inside. They walked up to the bar. The place was not too busy just then, and the bartender met them right away. "What'll it be, gents?" he asked.

"We're looking for a friend who came through here," said Old Jan. "Probably last night. Wearing a red shirt and a white hat."

"Tough-looking bastard," added Gourd.

"A man like that was here," the barkeep said. "He rode out south looking for three men. He didn't even stay long enough to have a drink."

"That's him," said Billy. "That's him for sure."

"Let's go after him then," said Old Jan.

"We have time for a drink," said Gourd.

"What'll it be?"

"Three whiskeys," said Gourd.

"We really ought to be going," said Old Jan.

"Hell," said Gourd, "Slocum never waits for us, does he? He don't think he needs us. Let's have a drink, and then we'll hit the trail again."

"Makes sense to me," said Billy.

"Well, you two do what you want," said Old Jan. "I'm riding on."

The bartender had already put a bottle and three glasses on the bar. He took the third glass back and poured two glasses full. Old Jan turned to walk outside.

"We'll catch up with you, old man," said Gourd. "Likely before you catch up with Slocum."

Old Jan mounted up and rode south out of town. He rode easy, watching the sign. A few miles out, he thought he recognized the prints of Slocum's big Appaloosa. Then he saw tracks of three horses coming along behind Slocum. He wondered about that. Could the three men they were after have gotten behind Slocum? He did not think so, but anything was possible. He recalled what Shakespeare's Hamlet had said: "There are more things in heaven and on earth than are dreamt of in your philosophy." He kept riding. After a while, he came to a spot in the road where the three riders had stopped. They had dismounted, and one of them had stood beside a boulder. He was at the top of a hill looking down on the road.

Then Old Jan got a big surprise. Down below, Slocum's Appaloosa came trotting along the road from the south. It stopped there where the land dropped off sharply on the east side of the road. Something was dreadfully wrong, Old Jan thought. He hurried his mount down the hill and stopped beside the Appaloosa. He dismounted. Walking up to the horse, he touched its muzzle.

"Hey, there, old boy," he said. "What's happened? Where's your pard?"

The Appaloosa whinnied and bobbed its head up and down. Old Jan then noticed something on the Appaloosa's saddle. He reached out and touched it. Bringing his hand back close to his face, he looked at his fingers. "Blood," he said. He looked around and saw nothing. The tracks of the three horses continued south. He walked to the edge and looked over, but he could see nothing.

"Slocum?" he called out.

There was no answer. He called again. Still deadly silence. But the big Appaloosa still stood there. Jan was sure that Slocum had been shot and had fallen over the side. The horse had run off after the shot, but had returned to where Slocum had gone over. Old Jan studied the drop-off carefully. It went down a long way, but there were places that could have stopped a fall. Slocum, or his body, could be out of sight along the way down. Jan decided he had to go down and look. It would be a dangerous climb. If he were not very careful, he could fall to his own death. But Slocum might be down there somewhere, and he might be alive. Even if he were not alive, Old Jan thought that he should bring back the body. He thought about how Slocum rode casually away from dead bodies, leaving them for the scavengers or for others to take care of. It was ironic that he should have someone to look after him—or his remains.

Old Jan took the rope off his saddle and tied it firmly around a boulder. He tested it. He was sure it would hold. He started to wrap it around his waist in preparation for the descent, but then stopped. How would he get Slocum back to the top? He went back to the Appaloosa and got Slocum's rope. He tied it to the same boulder and tossed it over the edge. Then he wrapped his own rope around his waist, turned his back to the drop-off, and started easing himself over the edge.

His first few steps were sure, and then he slipped, but he hung on tight to his rope and only banged himself against the side of the drop-off. He regained his footing and started the slow descent again. It was difficult going. At last he came to a small ledge, and he stopped to get his breath and to figure his next step, only to see Slocum snugged up tight against the wall of rocks. Jan moved cautiously to where Slocum lay. There was no movement. He pressed his head against Slocum's chest, and he could detect a heartbeat and shallow breathing. He also could feel sticky blood on Slocum's chest. He had lost considerable blood. Old Jan had no time to lose.

He dragged Slocum out closer to the edge of the shelf and grasped Slocum's rope, which was dangling there. Struggling with Slocum's deadweight, Old Jan managed to get the rope around the body under the arms, and he tied it securely.

Then he positioned Slocum as best he could to be dragged up the rough rock wall.

"Just hold on there, partner," he said to Slocum. Then he took hold of his own rope, still tied around his waist, and started the climb back to the top. It was slow, and it was a tough climb. He slipped twice, but he managed to hang on. At last, he struggled back up onto the ground beside the road. The Appaloosa neighed a greeting. Old Jan got to his feet and heaved a few heavy breaths.

"I found him, horse," he said. "We'll get him up here all right."

He moved to the boulder around which he had tied the ropes. He took his own rope off from around his waist and pulled it up, tossing it on the ground. Then he took hold of Slocum's rope and started to pull. He did not have the strength. He thought for a moment. Then he untied the rope from the boulder, and moved quickly to the Appaloosa. He lapped the rope around the saddle horn and secured it. Taking hold of the reins close to the horse's head, he started moving it backward.

"Come on, big horse," he said. "Let's get him up here. Come on now."

The Appaloosa moved back slowly, as if he understood Old Jan. He backed up to the center of the road and then almost to the other side. Old Jan looked back over his shoulder, watching for Slocum to appear over the edge. All he could see was the rope tightly stretched. There was no more room for backing up. He started moving north along the side of the road. He wondered how Slocum was faring, being dragged along the rugged, rocky side of the drop-off. He was bound to come up scratched and bruised in addition to the way he was when he'd landed down below. There was nothing for it, though. He had to be brought up. Then Slocum's head appeared over the edge. Old Jan rejoiced.

"We've got him, boy," he said to the Appaloosa. "Come on now. Bring him on over."

He backed the horse up some more. Just then he heard the

sound of horses coming. He hoped that it would be help. It could be the opposite.

"Whoa," he said. "Stand still."

The horse obeyed. Old Jan pulled the Remington revolver out of his holster and cocked it. Hunkered behind the Appaloosa, he waited. When he saw Gourd and Pierce come riding along, he eased the hammer back down and put the gun away. The two rode on up.

"What the hell?" said Gourd.

"It's about time you two shaggy-headed bastards showed up," Old Jan said. "Get him up over there."

The two looked toward the end of the rope and saw Slocum's head.

"Is he alive?" said Gourd.

"Just barely," Old Jan said. "Get him up."

Gourd and Pierce dismounted and hurried over to Slocum. Old Jan stayed where he was and kept the rope taut. Gourd took hold of Slocum by one arm and Pierce by the other. They pulled him up over the edge and laid him out flat. Old Jan unwound the rope from the Appaloosa's saddle horn. Then he rushed across the road to where Slocum lay and untied the rope that was around him.

"He's been shot," said Gourd.

"What other brilliant observation have you got?" asked Old Jan. "Get him up into my saddle."

The three of them managed to heave Slocum up, drag his leg across the horse, and then hold him in position in the saddle. Old Jan climbed on behind him and held him. "Let's go," he said.

"Where we going?" said Gourd.

"Back to North Fork," said Old Jan. "Where else?"

The ride back was slow. Old Jan was afraid of jostling Slocum around too much. He hoped and prayed along the way that they would find a doctor in North Fork. He hoped and prayed that Slocum would last that long. He needed attention, and he needed it soon. He was in a bad way.

"How'd it happen?" Pierce asked as they rode along.

"I don't know," Old Jan said. "I just found him like that.

His horse was standing there by the side of the road. There was blood on the saddle. I went over to look for him. You know the rest."

"He must have caught up to them and got the worst of it," Gourd said.

"I don't think so," said Old Jan. "He was shot in the back. It looked to me like they got behind him some way and then bushwhacked him."

"Oh," said Gourd. "Well, say, why don't I ride ahead and locate a doc for you?"

"That's a good idea," said Old Jan.

Gourd kicked his horse in the sides and raced off. Old Jan looked at Pierce.

"I'll stick with you," Billy said, "in case you need any help with him."

Old Jan was a patient rider, but he did not usually have a nearly dead friend in the saddle in front of him. All the way back to North Fork he worried that they might not make it in time. He worried if North Fork would have a doctor, and if it did, if he would be worth a shit. At last they made it, though, and Old Jan thought that Slocum was still breathing. As they rode into town, Gourd was sitting in his saddle in the middle of the road. He waved at them.

"This way," he said.

He led the way to a small building a few doors down from the Watering Hole Saloon. They tied their horses and eased Slocum down out of the saddle. The doc, having been alerted by Gourd, saw them and opened the door. As they carried Slocum in, the doc indicated a table, and they laid Slocum out on it.

"Do what you can for him, Doc," said Old Jan.

The doctor looked at Slocum. He examined the wound.

"One of you men run across the street to that little yellow house and tell my nurse to get over here. She's there by herself."

"I'll go," said Billy. He hurried out the door.

"I'll be a while at this," the doc said. "You men might just as well go have a drink or get yourselves a room for the night. Get out of my way."

The two looked at each other, and Old Jan nodded toward the door. They left the doctor's office. Outside, they stood for a moment on the sidewalk. A good-looking young woman came running from the house across the street followed by Billy. The woman hurried on inside, and Billy stopped on the sidewalk with Old Jan and Gourd. "What're we going to do?" he said.

"Get us a room and then get something to eat," said Old Jan.

"We can't do anything more for Slocum," said Gourd. "I say we go on after them three bastards before they get too far ahead."

"I'm staying here with him," said Old Jan.

"No sense in three of us staying here," said Gourd. "I'm going after them. What about you, Billy?"

Billy looked from Gourd to Old Jan. He looked back at Gourd. "I'll ride with you," he said.

"Well, then," said Old Jan, "good luck to you boys."

"Yeah," said Billy. "The same to you and to Slocum."

The two mounted up and rode out of town going south. Old Jan watched them go. Then he looked up and down the street for a hotel. Spotting one, he walked down there leading his horse and Slocum's Appaloosa. He went inside and got a room, asked for a livery stable and got directions, then took the horses to the livery. He walked down the street again till he came to a small café, where he went in for a meal. Having finished the meal, he walked to the Watering Hole. He went inside and bought a bottle. The barkeep gave him a glass as well, and Old Jan stood at the bar to drink.

"Say," said the barkeep. "Wasn't you here before with two buddies?"

"I was," said Old Jan.

"I thought you was riding out looking for someone. You give up so soon?"

"I found him," said Old Jan. "He'd been bushwhacked. Brought him back to the doctor."

"That's too bad. How is he?"

"It's too soon to tell. He's tough, though."

"He was after three men, wasn't he?"

"That's right. I think they got behind him."

"I'd bet they was in here when he was," the barkeep said in a low voice.

"What makes you say that?"

"Well, earlier, one man come in here by himself. Stood right here having a drink. A little later, two more men come in and sat over yonder. In a while, the two went upstairs with Bitsy there. Then your pard came in asking about three men. The one here at the bar told him that he seen three men heading south out of town. Your pard left after them. Then the man that had told him that story hurried upstairs, and he came back down with those other two. They left out of here in a hurry."

"Did you hear any names?" Old Jan asked.

"Nope, but Bitsy might have." He looked around the room and spied her. Raising his voice, he called out, "Bitsy. Come over here." Bitsy looked in his direction. Then she made an excuse to the cowboy she was talking to and walked over to see what the barkeep wanted.

"What is it, Mike?" she asked. "I got a live one over there."

"This will just take a minute," Mike the barkeep said. "You remember those two you took upstairs together?"

"How could I forget?" she said.

"Did you get their names?"

"Names?" she said. "Who cares about names? A couple of drifters. Wait a minute. Wait. One of them was called Jigs. I remember that one. A funny name. Jigs."

Old Jan pulled a bill out of his pocket and handed it to Bitsy. "Thanks," he said.

She looked at the bill and a broad smile spread across her face. "Thank you, mister," she said. "Is that all you want to know?"

"That's it," said Old Jan. Bitsy turned and went back to her cowboy. Old Jan pulled out another bill and handed it to the barkeep. "And thank you, sir."

"Glad to be of assistance," Mike said. "So, are they the ones?"

"Just as sure as hell," Old Jan said. "They're the ones."

5

Sluice sat in a poker game in the small town of Jones Mill some miles south of North Fork. He was in a saloon and gambling hall called simply The Place. He was winning big. Hardy and Jigs were sitting at a table sharing a bottle of whiskey. Hardy always lost when he gambled, so he decided to stay out of the game. Jigs did not even know how to play the game. But Sluice was mighty lucky at cards, or maybe he was a slick cheat. Whatever the truth, he was winning.

One shrewd gambler dropped out of the game saying that he was damn near cleaned out. More likely, he realized that Sluice was probably cheating him, but he didn't want to fight, figuring that Sluice was a tough and mean son of a bitch. So he cut his losses and got out while the getting was good. There were still a cowpoke, a businessman, and a traveling salesman at the table. They played another hand, and Sluice scraped up the winnings again.

"By God," he said, "the luck's with me today. I ain't had a streak like this in a fucking coon's age."

"Your luck's got to play out sooner or later," said the salesman. "Deal the cards."

Sluice dealt another round, and each man picked up his cards and held them close to his face. The cowpoke called

36

for two cards, the businessman for one, and the salesman held on to what he had. Sluice held his. They made their bets and Sluice called. The businessman laid down his cards, a weak hand. The salesman put his down. It was a little better. The cowpoke put down his cards and grinned a wide grin.

"Beat that, by God," he said.

Sluice smiled a sly smile and laid down his cards. "How's that?" he said. He reached for the pot to scrape it in.

"Your luck couldn't be that good," said the cowpoke. "I say you've been cheating."

"Either take that back or back it up," said Sluice.

"You son of a bitch," said the cowpoke, reaching for his six-gun. Sluice's revolver was out in a flash, and he blasted a hole in the man's chest. The cowpoke was dead on his feet, but he staggered back a few steps to sprawl across the table in between Hardy and Jigs.

"Goddamn," said Hardy. Jigs grabbed the bottle just in time to save it. "Damn, Sluice," he said. "Couldn't you have killed him in another direction?"

The two got up and moved to another table. Sluice kept his shooter in his hand and looked at the remaining players. The salesman put his hands up and shrugged. The businessman spread his arms wide. "The cowboy pulled his gun first," he said. Sluice looked around the room. No one else said anything or made a move. Sluice holstered his weapon and finished scraping up his winnings.

Just then a man with a badge on his chest stepped into the room. He looked around and spotted the body still laid out on the table. He walked over to look at it. "Dead, huh?" he said. "Who did the shooting?"

"I did," said Sluice. "It was self-defense."

The sheriff looked around, and several men nodded their agreement. "That's right," said the businessman. "The cowboy drew first."

"That's right," said the salesman.

Over at the bar, the gambler who had dropped out earlier spoke up, too. "The cowpoke was a sore loser," he said.

"All right then," the sheriff said, but he gave Sluice a hard look. "If I was you, though, I'd get the hell out of town."

"Funny thing, Your Honor," said Sluice, "I was just thinking about that myself. It ain't too friendly a town any-how."

He poured himself another drink and downed it. Then he turned to his two cronies. "Come on," he said. "Let's get out of this goddamn one-horse town."

Jigs and Hardy stood up, Jigs picking up the bottle, which was still about half full. On the way out of The Place, Sluice stopped and bought two more bottles. The three of them walked out of The Place and mounted up. They rode out of town, still headed south, actually a little southwest. As they rode, Jigs and Hardy drank from their bottle, passing it back and forth. Sluice reached out and took the bottle, taking a long drink before handing it back to Jigs.

"How far we riding, Sluice?" asked Hardy.

"I ain't sure," Sluice said. "I'm breaking new ground here. Don't know how far it is to the next town."

"Say, how much money did you make back there?" asked Jigs.

"Never mind that," Sluice said. "I made enough all right. We'll get along just fine for a spell, wherever we land up."

Gourd and Pierce rode into Jones Mill. It was a small place with only one saloon, so they rode up to the front of The Place, tied their horses, and went inside. They ordered a drink at the bar. When the barkeep poured their drinks, Gourd said, "Do you have a sheriff in this town?"

"He's sitting right over there at that table," said the bar-keep.

Gourd looked, and saw a man sitting alone at a far table. There was a badge on his chest. Gourd picked up his drink and walked over to that table, followed by Pierce. The sher-iff looked up.

"Howdy," said Gourd.

"Something I can do for you?" said the sheriff.

"We're trailing three men," said Gourd.

"Killers," said Pierce.

"Killers, you say?"

"The boss of the bunch is called Sluice. He killed a man in Cheyenne and was set to hang. His pals, names of Jigs and Hardy, busted him out. Then they murdered our boss, Trent Brady. There was four of us set out after them, but they ambushed our pard, name of Slocum. Our other pal stayed back in North Fork with him, waiting for him to heal up, I guess. Anyhow, now it's just two of us after them."

"Killed Trent Brady, huh? I knew old Trent. He was a good man."

"The best," said Pierce.

"Yeah," agreed the sheriff. "Well, I expect your bunch was here, all right. Man named Sluice killed a cowpoke who objected to his poker-playing techniques. I told him and the others to get out of town. You're not too far behind them."

"They head south out of town?" asked Gourd.

"The only way they could go if you didn't pass them on your way in."

Back in North Fork, Old Jan went back to the doctor's office. When he went in, he saw Slocum still laid out on the table, still sleeping or unconscious or whatever he was. The doc looked up when Old Jan came in. "How is he, Doc?" Old Jan asked.

"Not much change," said Doc. "I can say this. He'll live. He's a tough one all right. He'll come around, but I don't have any idea how long it'll be."

"Well, how much do I owe you?" said Old Jan.

"Never mind that till he gets up and around," Doc said. "That is, if you intend on hanging around till then."

"I'll be around," Old Jan said. On his way out the door, he met the young nurse coming in. He tipped his hat to her and went on his way.

Night was falling when Sluice decided they better stop along the trail to sleep. He still had no idea how far it was to the next town. He chose a spot where the road, which wasn't much more than a trail at that point, ran alongside a clear mountain stream. He ordered Jigs to take care of the horses and Hardy to build a fire. He sat down with his back against a tree and opened up one of his bottles to take a long drink.

"Hurry up with that fire, Hardy," he said. "It's getting chilly tonight."

"I'm moving as fast as I can, Sluice."

"Well, get the lead out."

Finished with the horses, Jigs walked over to Sluice and sat down. "Can I have a pull on that jug?" he asked.

"Help Hardy get that fire going," Sluice said.

Jigs got down on his knees in front of the small pile of sticks Hardy had gotten together. He struck a match and tried to get the fire going. Hardy was still gathering wood. It took them a while, but they finally got a small fire going. Sluice told them to gather more wood. He didn't allow them to stop till they had a good blaze going. "Stack up plenty of wood there," he said, "so you can keep it going all night. I don't want to wake up freezing my ass off."

"I sure do wish we had come to another town," said Jigs.

"Well," said Sluice, "we didn't, so there ain't no sense crying about it."

"Hell," said Jigs, "I ain't crying about it. I just wish we'd of come to one. That's all."

"You don't even know what the next town will be like," said Hardy. "It might be a dump, for all you know."

"Even a dump would be better than this. I ain't cut out for trail life. I belong in a big city."

"You'd be hanging out in the damn slums," said Hardy.

"I'd rather be in the slums than out here," said Jigs.

"Come on over here, boys," Sluice said, "and have a drink."

"Well, yes, by God, I will," said Hardy.

"'Bout time," muttered Jigs.

"What's that?" said Sluice.

"I said, 'That's fine,'" Jigs declared, covering up for what he had really said.

The three of them got drunk, and finally fell asleep or passed out. The sun was up in the sky before they woke up. They woke up hungry, but they did not have anything to eat with them, so Sluice ordered them to pack up. They rode off, still headed south, with the ashes from their fire still smoldering.

"How far's the next town?" Jigs asked.

"I done told you," said Sluice, "I ain't got no idea."

Gourd and Pierce came across the still-smoldering ashes. They stopped and looked around at the campsite.

"I'd say it was them all right," said Gourd.

"How can you tell?" Pierce asked.

"Well," said Gourd, "there was three horses for sure. Then they built a great big fire like the assholes they are. They didn't put it out when they left either. And look here. An empty whiskey bottle."

"There's all kinds of men might be guilty of all that," Pierce said.

"The main thing," said Gourd, "is that their tracks are the most recent ones to come out of James Mill."

"Jones Mill," said Pierce.

"What?"

"The place is named Jones Mill."

"That's what I said. Anyhow, these tracks are the last ones out of there."

"Yeah," Pierce said. "I reckon you're right about that for sure. How far ahead of us you reckon they are?"

Old Jan stopped back in the doc's office. This time he found Slocum awake. Doc looked at Old Jan and scowled. "Don't tire him out," he said.

The nurse smiled at Old Jan and said in a low voice, "Don't worry. He's all right for a visit. I think it might even do him some good."

"Thank you, ma'am," said Old Jan. "Slocum, pard, I'm glad to find you awake. I was worried you might not come out of it."

"I'll be out of here in no time," Slocum said. "Hey, by the way, how the hell did I get here?"

"Oh, I found you out on the road. Back-shot."

"Yeah," said Slocum, "I remember now. But I wasn't on the road. I was down the side. In fact, I was where no one from up on the road could see me."

"Oh, well," said Old Jan. "I came across your faithful steed hanging around right where you went off."

"So you went down the side looking for me?" Slocum asked.

"Well, yeah. I guess I did."

Slocum smiled. "I reckon I owe you," he said.

"Aw, it wasn't so much trouble."

"No," said Slocum. "I guess not. Where are Gourd and Pierce?"

"They decided to keep after Sluice and them," Old Jan said. "I said I'd wait here with you."

"Well," Slocum said, "we'll catch up with them."

"You won't catch up with anyone," said the doctor in a grumpy voice. "Not unless they sit still and wait for you for a spell."

"I'll be out of here in no time," Slocum said again.

"No, you won't," said Doc. Then he turned to Old Jan. "But you will. Right now. He needs his rest. Get out of here now. Get."

Old Jan looked at the nurse. She gave him a look and a shrug.

Gourd and Pierce had ridden all night. Topping a rise, they spotted three riders down below, not far ahead of them on the road. They stopped and looked at each other.

"That's them," said Gourd.

"Are you sure?" Pierce asked.

"Hell, yes," said Gourd. "Remember? We've seen no other tracks on the road but the tracks from that campsite."

"Well, yeah. So, what're we going to do?"

"Let them ride over that next rise. Then let's hurry along

to the top of the rise. We'll be closer if we do that. There's boulders up there. We'll dismount and hunker down and then pop off at them with our rifles. We ought to get all three of them easy."

"I don't know about that," Pierce said. "I ain't never yet shot anyone without giving them fair warning and an even chance."

"These are killers," said Gourd.

"I know that. I wouldn't be after them at all if they wasn't. I still ain't gunning them down from behind without no warning."

"All right. All right," said Gourd, his voice exasperated. "We'll yell at them before we start shooting. Does that satisfy you?"

"Yeah," said Pierce. "I reckon that will be all right."

When Sluice and the others disappeared over the next rise, Gourd and Pierce whipped up their mounts. They raced the rest of the way down the hill and then up the next one, hauling back on their reins just before they would have reached the top. They dismounted, secured their horses, and took places behind the big boulders with their rifles in hand.

"I've got a damn good shot from here," said Gourd, raising his rifle to his shoulder.

"Wait a minute, Charlie," said Pierce. "Remember what you agreed to."

"All right. Shit," said Gourd. "Hey, you, Sluice," he yelled. "Sluice and you two other goat shits."

The three riders down below halted their mounts and looked around. Sluice turned his horse clear around.

"Who is that?" he called out.

"Never mind who," said Gourd. "We mean to kill you. That's all."

Sluice lowered his voice. "Take cover, boys," he said.

While Jigs and Hardy dismounted and ran for the side of the road, Sluice ran his horse off the side of the road, then turned and raced south. As he did so, he spooked the other two horses, and they, too, ran south. Jigs and Hardy turned to watch them go.

"The son of a bitch run out on us," said Jigs.

"Yeah," said Hardy. "Well, we'll deal with him later. Right now we got them up yonder to worry about."

6

Billy Pierce fired an overanxious shot that went wide of its mark, missing Jigs by several feet and harmlessly kicking up dirt. Jigs scrunched down behind a small boulder on the west side of the road. Hardy flattened himself there beside the road and tried to look up to see who was firing at him. He could not see the top of the rise from his position, so he got to his feet again, staying in a crouched position, and ran for a nearby tree, securing himself behind its trunk.

"Do you see them, Jigs?" he called out.

"No, I can't see shit."

Gourd fired a shot that chipped the boulder behind which Jigs was snugged.

"Yikes," yelped Jigs.

Hardy saw where the shot had come from, and he fired off a round that came within a few feet of Gourd.

"You got them spotted now, Billy?" Gourd asked.

"I think I know where two of them are," said Billy, "but I can't get a clear shot at them."

"One's behind that big tree yonder," said Gourd. "The other one's behind that little boulder a few feet on past him."

"That's what I figured. How do we get at them?"

"Just wait for one to show himself," Gourd said. "Then pick him off."

"I think if I move up just a bit," Billy said, "I can get a better angle on them."

"Go ahead," Gourd said. "Try it."

Billy looked up. He and Gourd were behind a huge pile of boulders. He inched himself around until he found a place where he could climb. He made his way up slowly to the next boulder and took another look. He could not see at all. Maybe he had been wrong. He tried going up even farther and found himself behind an even larger rock. He straightened himself up as best he could and peered over the top of the big rock. He could see what looked like an ass sticking out from behind the big tree trunk. He raised his rifle, cocked it, and put it to his shoulder. He took careful aim and fired. He could see blood splatter from the target.

"Ow. Yow," Hardy screamed. "Oh. Goddamn it."

"You hit?" said Jigs.

"Son of a bitch shot me in the ass," yelled Hardy. "Oh. Son of a bitch. Goddamn. My ass. My ass."

Up on the hill, Gourd said, "Good shot, Billy. You got one of them."

"I just shot his butt," said Billy. "He can still handle his rifle."

"That's all right," Gourd said. "I bet it hurts like hell."

Back in North Fork, Slocum was lying awake on the table. Time was wasting, he thought. He moved his arms, getting his hands on the edge of the table at his sides, and he heaved to sit up. "Ah," he groaned. He paused, took a deep breath, and pushed again. This time he managed to sit up. He sat there breathing deeply for a long moment. Doc was in the back room doing whatever doctors do alone. Slocum was hurting. He began to wonder if he should have tried getting up. He thought about lying down again and trying later. Just then the door to the outside opened, jingling the bell that hung up at the top. Old Jan stepped in, and Doc came in from the back room to see who was coming into his office.

"Slocum," said Old Jan. "What're you—"

"What the hell are you doing up?" Doc said.

"I ain't quite up," Slocum said.

"Since you're feeling so perky," said Doc, "and since we've got some help here, we'll just move you to the bed."

"I don't see no bed," Slocum said.

"It's in the back room," Doc said. "Take his left arm," he added to Old Jan. Old Jan took Slocum by his left arm and Doc took him by his right. "Come on now," Doc said.

They pulled Slocum off the table. As soon as his feet hit the floor, his knees buckled. Doc and Old Jan almost dropped him, but they managed to hold him up, and he managed to tighten up his legs and stand up. The sudden movement shot pains through his body, and he groaned out loud.

"You all right, Slocum?" asked Old Jan.

"Of course, he's all right," Doc grumbled. "Now, walk to the door."

Taking slow and painful steps, with Doc and Old Jan holding him up, Slocum managed to make it to the door. It was standing open, and they got through it all right. The bed was against the far wall, and they walked Slocum across the room. They turned him so that he could sit on the edge. Then Doc pushed him over onto his back and lifted his legs up. Slocum groaned, and then heaved a long and heavy sigh.

"More comfy?" asked Doc.

"It feels pretty good," Slocum said. "How much longer will I have to be here?"

"Whatever you think you've got to do," said Doc, "just put it out of your mind. Relax and heal yourself up."

Doc walked back across the room to a cabinet and got a pill. Then he poured a glass of water from a pitcher that stood against the wall. He carried the glass and the pill to Slocum and made him take the pill and wash it down with water. Then he went to his desk and sat down. Old Jan watched him for a moment, until he was satisfied that Doc was finished for the time being. Then he grabbed a chair and pulled it over to Slocum's bedside.

"Are you feeling a little better?" he asked.

"A little, I guess," Slocum said. "I tried to get up a while ago. Reckon it was a little soon. I need to get out of here before that damn Sluice leaves the country or something."

"Don't worry about that," said Old Jan. "The boys are on his trail. Hell, by the time we catch up with them, they'll likely have killed him already."

"I don't want the boys to kill him, Jan," Slocum said. "I want to do that myself."

Just then, the nurse stepped into the room. She heard what Slocum said, and she stepped over to the bed.

"Are you so anxious to get back to killing?" she asked him.

"In this case," he said, "I am."

"Well, I'm afraid you'll have to exercise your patience," she said.

"You know," said Slocum, looking at her really for the first time and taking note of her rather appealing appearance, "we ain't never really been introduced. My name's Slocum, and this here is my pard, Old Jan."

"I'm pleased to meet you, ma'am," Old Jan said, standing.

"My name is Jill McGee," the nurse said. "I work with Dr. Harman here."

"Now," said Slocum, "that's better. It might even make it easier for me to—what did you say?—exercise my patience."

"Jigs," said Hardy. "Jigs."

"What?" answered Jigs.

"Jigs, we got to kill them two up there. Is it two?"

"I think it's just two," said Jigs.

"Well, we got to kill them real soon somehow. I'm bleeding to death here through a hole in my ass cheek."

"Well, I can't see them," said Jigs.

"All right," said Hardy. "We'll just shoot a bunch up there and see if we can't spook them out. Now."

Hardy began firing his rifle as fast as he could, and Jigs joined in. Bullets bounced off the boulders around Pierce and Gourd, causing them both to stay low behind their protective rocks. Bits of rock were showered over their heads.

Then all at once, the shooting stopped. Gourd popped up first to shoot back, and then Pierce. Hardy hugged his tree trunk, his butt still bleeding. Jigs practically dug a hole behind his boulder. In a short while, the shooting stopped again. No one was any better off.

"Jigs?" said Hardy.

"What is it now?" said Jigs.

"Jigs, can you see our horses?"

Jigs twisted his neck a little to look south on the road. "They're down there a little ways," he said, "grazing along the side of the road like there's nothing wrong."

"Can you get to them?"

"Without getting shot to pieces, you mean?"

"Can you?"

"Well, maybe I can," Jigs said, "if I sneak along on the side of the road here."

"Get to them and bring them back here. We'll mount up and get the hell out of here."

Jigs started to ask Hardy if he was nuts. He could maybe get to the horses, but it would be suicide to bring them back down the road to where Hardy would be waiting with his bloody ass. And how fast could the silly bastard mount up with that extra hole in his ass? And what was Jigs supposed to be doing in the meantime? Sitting there in the middle of the road waiting patiently for him, posing there for those goddamn shooters up on top of the hill? He started to say all that, but he changed his mind.

"Okay," he said. He moved a little farther away from the road to get himself more out of sight of the shooters up above. Then he started working his way between the boulders and the trees and through the brush to the place up ahead where the horses grazed. He reached it safely at last. He crept back to the edge of the road and peered cautiously toward the top of hill. He was out of its sight. He moved out onto the road easily toward the horses. His own mount neighed and trotted farther away.

"Goddamn you," Jigs said. "Both of you. Make out like nothing's wrong here."

He moved in on Hardy's horse, and it let him walk right up. He shoved his rifle in the boot and swung up into the saddle. Then he turned the horse south and started riding away from where Hardy waited, hiding behind his tree, bleeding from the ass. As Jigs rode past his own horse, he took off his hat and waved it and slapped at the horse, turning it north and sending it scurrying. Then he rode on.

"There," he said to himself, "I've sent him a goddamn horse. That's all I can do."

Jigs raced south along the road, his head full of fresh worries. What if Hardy managed somehow to survive, to get on the horse with his bloody ass, and come riding after him? He would be mad as hell for sure. Jigs wasn't at all sure he could take Hardy, even with his ass shot. He would have to watch his back trail all right, for Hardy or for the other two, and he wasn't at all sure what the other two looked like. So there were two or possibly three behind him, all of whom would be out to kill him. And what if he outran all of them and came upon Sluice? That just might be the worst thing that could happen. What would he say to Sluice? Would Sluice even give him a chance to say anything?

He wondered if there was another direction he could ride. He knew he couldn't ride west because of the mountains. What would happen if he turned east? Would he find a trail or a road anywhere? If he tried it, would he get himself hopelessly lost? He even thought about turning around and going back to help Hardy. But he rejected that idea. There were several dangers ahead of him, but that one was the nearest. He would continue running from it.

Hardy saw Jigs's horse come running up the road. It moved right past him and climbed the hill. There was no sign of his own horse or of Jigs. Jigs had either fucked up royally or had double-crossed him. There was no other explanation. He thought hard. He wondered what to do. He realized that he was alone against two men who meant to kill him. He was on foot, and he was wounded. He had few options.

He could wait it out behind this tree and continue bleeding

until he passed out from the loss of blood, passed out or died. He could step out into the road and shoot until the two up above killed him, which they would surely do under these circumstances. Or he could try crawling into the wilderness to the east. He had no idea what he would find out there. Suddenly, tears started streaming down his face. He knew it was the end. He cranked a shell into the chamber of his rifle and limped out into the road. He fired at the boulders at the top of the rise. He cranked another shell and fired again. He continued firing like that until the rifle was empty.

He flung the rifle aside and drew out his revolver, wondering why there was no return fire. He raised the six-gun to shoot at the same spot above, and just then a man appeared from behind a boulder. Hardy fired his weapon, but the range was too great for a good shot. The man above put a rifle to his shoulder and fired, and Hardy felt a burning pain shoot through his chest. He staggered and fell back, landing hard in the dirt. He drew a last, jerky, gurgling breath, and then he breathed no more.

Up above, Gourd looked down on what he had done. No more shots came from below, even though he was absolutely exposed.

"Charlie," said Pierce, "get down."

"Hell," said Gourd, "no one's shooting."

"But there's another one down there. We know there was two of them."

"The other one must have got away somehow," said Gourd, "Let's mount up and go on down and see."

They were down the hill in a few minutes, still holding their guns ready in case the other man was still lurking somewhere. Gourd dismounted and nudged Hardy's corpse with his boot toe. He picked up the rifle and the six-gun and handed them to Pierce. Then he knelt beside the body and went through the pockets. He found a wad of money and pocketed it.

"Should you be doing that?" said Billy.

"Why not?" said Gourd.

"Well, I—"

"It ain't going to do him no good in hell," Gourd said.

"No. I guess not. Well, the other one's gone just like you said."

"Yeah," said Gourd, standing up and looking around. He bent down to take hold of the body by one leg and started dragging it out of the road. "One horse run past us. There's no sign of the other one. He got to it somehow and took off." He rolled the body off the road a ways. "We'd best get after him."

"Him and the third one," said Billy.

"Yeah. There's still two to go," said Gourd. "Won't Slocum be surprised when we go back and tell him we got all of them? Him all laid up and hurt like he is."

"Yeah. I reckon he will," Billy said.

Up ahead, Jigs was still worrying about what might happen next. He came to a spot in the road that struck him as the perfect place for an ambush. It was a large outcropping of rock that stuck out almost into the road at the bottom, and rose up high at the top. There was room on the south side to hide a horse, and there the hillside looked easy enough to climb. He made a quick decision. He rode around to the south side of the rock and dismounted. He tied his horse there, not wanting to take another chance on losing it. He took the rifle from the boot and started climbing. It was a more difficult climb than he had anticipated, but at last he made it to the top of the rock.

He settled himself there in such a way as to prevent anyone riding down the road from seeing him, but at the same time allowing him a good view of the road to the north. He knew that someone would be following him before long. One or both of the two mysterious shooters or Hardy. Either way, he would be ready for them. He cranked a shell into the chamber of his rifle and prepared himself for a shot. He wished they would hurry up. He was ready for a kill. Hell, he needed one.

Gourd and Pierce rode south in silence for a space. At last Pierce spoke up. "You think it's all right to just leave him lay there like that? Food for the coyotes? I know Slocum left that first one like that, but I ain't sure—"

"Billy," said Gourd, in an exasperated voice, "if you want to bury the son of a bitch and pray over him, ride on back there and do it. I don't give a shit."

"I didn't say that," said Pierce. "I don't know. I just don't feel right about all this."

"You don't even have to ride along," Gourd said. "Why don't you just turn around and ride back to North Fork and wait for Slocum along with Old Jan? No one will think less about you for it. You just ain't got the stomach for this kind of killing is all. There ain't nothing wrong with that. People is made in different ways. That's all. Turn around and go on back. Hell, we're just following one man is all. Anyhow, one at a time."

Just then a rifle shot rang out, and a splotch of blood appeared in the center of Gourd's chest. His face took on a bewildered look. Then it went blank. The body slouched and then slid slowly from the saddle to land with a dull thud in the hard-packed earth of the road. A small puff of dust rose around it.

7

Billy wanted to dismount and see if he could help Gourd, but Gourd looked dead and the shooter was still out there. Billy turned his horse quickly and headed to the side of the road. He got out his rifle, cranked a shell into the chamber, and dismounted. He tried to get a look down the road. He spotted a high rock up ahead, and he figured the shooter was up there. Billy wasn't sure, but it looked to him like an ideal place. Then he saw a slight movement, brief, and whatever it was disappeared. He still waited. He heard a horse, and then he saw the man riding south fast. He was out of sight quickly before Billy could even put his rifle to his shoulder. He stepped out into the road and stared ahead for a moment. The killer was gone.

Billy walked over to the body of Gourd and knelt beside it. He was dead all right. Gourd had most likely been killed instantly. Billy put a hand on Gourd's forehead for an instant. He took the man's gun belt off and threw it over his shoulder. He fumbled in the pockets and took out the money that Gourd had taken off the body of the last one they had killed. He stuffed the money into his own pocket. Then he loaded the body across the saddle of what had been Gourd's horse only a few minutes ago. Taking the reins, he mounted his own horse and turned back north. He rode slowly.

Sluice had made it across the border into Nebraska, and he soon came to a small town called Bascomb. He located the one hotel, not a difficult task, tied his horse out front, and went inside to the desk. A sleepy-eyed clerk looked up and asked, "Room?"

"That's what you go into a hotel for, ain't it?" said Sluice.

"Sign the book," the clerk said.

Sluice picked up the pen, dipped it, and wrote, "Callendar."

The clerk took his money, tossed him a key, and said, "First door down the hall."

Sluice carried his gear down to the room and stashed it there. Then he walked back to the desk. "Where's the stable?" he demanded more than asked.

"Far end of the street," said the clerk.

"Saloon?"

"Two doors down."

Sluice walked outside again and mounted his horse. He rode to the livery and paid the man there to take care of the horse. He had taken note of the saloon on his way down to the stable, so he walked the short distance back to it and went inside. He walked to the bar and was met by a large bartender with a handlebar mustache.

"What's your pleasure?" the barkeep said.

"Whiskey," said Sluice.

The barkeep poured a drink, but as he started to put the bottle away, Sluice stopped him. "Leave it," he said, and he tossed some money on the bar.

"You're a stranger here," the barkeep said.

"I ain't surprised you noticed," Sluice said. "You only got a one-horse town here. One hotel. One saloon. One livery."

"One of each is plenty," the barkeep said. "Especially when one man owns them all."

"One man, eh?"

"That's right," said the big man.

"Who is he?" Sluice asked.

"Meet Tom Grimes," he said. "Me."

Sluice shook hands with Grimes and smiled wide.

"Well, sir," he said, "it's a real pleasure to meet a genuine enterprising man. The whole damn town, huh?"

"Yeah. That's right. I just got the last piece of property here. Man that owned the hardware store decided to get out. He sold me the place cheap."

"My name's Callendar," said Sluice, and they shook hands. "I don't suppose you'd like to unload that hardware store for a little more than what you paid for it?"

"Why? You interested?"

"I might be," said Sluice. "If the price is right."

"Well, now, why would I want to sell? I just got hold of the last place of business in this town. I own it all."

"How you going to run it all just all by your own self? Tell you what," said Sluice. "You keep the property and sell me the business. I'll pay you a cut of everything I make."

"You run a business like that before?" Grimes asked.

"Sure," Sluice lied. "I had me my own business up in Cheyenne. I sold it out a while back on account of business wasn't very good. There was two other such establishments in town. I always wanted a setup like this one here."

"All right," said Grimes. "Let's talk figures."

Billy Pierce rode slowly into Jones Mill leading Gourd's horse, which was bearing Gourd's body. He stopped in front of the sheriff's office and dismounted. The sheriff saw him through the window and came out onto the sidewalk.

"What's happened?" he asked.

"We caught up with them," said Pierce. "We got one, and the other one ran off. We went after him, but he laid an ambush. He killed Charlie."

"I thought you were following three men," the sheriff said.

"Seems like the leader—"

"Sluice?"

"Yeah. Him. Seems like he run out on the other two soon as we caught up with them."

"Well, let's take care of your friend."

The sheriff led the way to the undertaker's place, where Billy made the arrangements and paid the man. Then they walked back to the sheriff's office.

"I wish I could help you," the sheriff said. "But from what you said, they're out of my jurisdiction. What are your plans?"

"I don't know," said Billy. "I guess I'll ride back to North Fork and find Slocum and Old Jan. Tell them what's happened out here."

"Well, about all I can do is send out some wire messages to the towns south of here and let them know to watch for them. Good luck to you."

Jigs reached the border to Nebraska. There was a sign that said it was three miles to the town of Bascomb. He started to ride on, but he stopped, hesitated. Sluice might have stopped there, thinking that he was safe now in Nebraska. Jigs did not want to come upon Sluice unexpected, unexpected by either one or both of them. That could be very dangerous. He wondered what he could do. He rode on slowly until he was almost to Bascomb. He spotted a grove of trees off to the side of the road, and moved into them. He looked at the sun low in the sky. Soon it would be dark. He decided to stop there until it was full dark. Then he would ride on in slow and easy. If anyone was going to be surprised, he wanted it to be Sluice.

In town, Sluice, as Callendar, was just finishing up a round of drinks with Grimes in the saloon. They had signed a paper together, and Sluice had handed over a batch of money, stolen from the stagecoach, to Grimes. They had shaken hands and then had had several drinks together. Sluice told Grimes that he wanted to go take a look at the hardware store, and Grimes had given him the key to the front door.

"Help yourself," he said.

Sluice left the saloon, staggering slightly, and headed for the hardware store. He noted that it was dark already. At the edge of town, a lurking Jigs saw Sluice crossing the street. He smiled. Luck was with him this night. He eased himself into town, watching as Sluice unlocked the door to the store and walked in. Jigs tied his horse across the street from the store and dismounted. He stood for a moment watching while Sluice apparently found a lamp and lit it. Then he unholstered his six-gun, cocked it, and started walking toward the store.

When Sluice got the light lit, he held it up and looked around. He was pleased. He saw just about anything anybody could want. There were bolts of cloth. There were canned goods. There was candy on the counter. There were boxes of bullets of every caliber imaginable. There was a pickle barrel. There were trousers and shirts, belts, dresses, men's hats, and women's hats. Sluice wondered how there could be enough people around to buy all this stuff. Then it occurred to him that there might not be. Maybe that was why Grimes had been so easy to deal with. Maybe Grimes had played him for a sucker. Or thought that he had. Sluice had a trick or two up his sleeve yet. He went to the cash register and opened it. The cash drawer was empty except for a few coins. Disgusted, he slammed it shut again.

He turned around to examine the shelves behind the counter, and when he did, he heard the front door open. He turned again to see Jigs standing there with his six-gun in his hand. The pistol was pointed generally at Sluice's middle. Sluice spread his hands out wide. "Jigs," he said. "I'm glad you're here."

"Sure you are, you dirty son of a bitch," said Jigs.

"What?" said Sluice. "What is this? You mean to kill me?"

"You damn right," said Jigs. "You run out on us. Hardy went and got hisself killed."

"I'm sorry to hear that," said Sluice. "Hell, I figured you two could handle them all right. I kept looking over my shoulder expecting to see the both of you riding up behind me to say you'd killed them all. What went wrong?"

Jigs's face developed a puzzled expression. Here was an unexpected wrinkle.

"I scouted ahead to make sure there weren't no surprises waiting for us up that way while you two took care of that little problem behind us," said Sluice. "I been expecting you, well, both of you, for quite some time now."

Jigs wrinkled his brow. "You, uh, you telling me the truth?" he asked. "You ain't lying to me?"

"Why the hell would I lie to you, Jigs?" said Sluice. "Why, hell, we're pardners, ain't we? Didn't you and Hardy break me out of jail? Didn't you save my ass from a hanging? Why, Jigs, I owe you for just about everything."

"Ham helped us break you out of jail," said Jigs. "I remember how you run out on him."

"Ham was hurt and so was his horse. There was men on our trail. If we had stopped to help Ham, they'd have got us all. It was that simple, Jigs. I hated doing it, but there just wasn't no choice. Can you see that?"

"Well, yeah," said Jigs, lowering his pistol a bit. "I reckon I can see it."

"Come on in here," said Sluice, "and look over my new setup."

"Your—"

"This whole store is mine now," Sluice said. "And you can come in on it with me."

"Me? And you?"

"That's right, pard. It's all ours."

"But, hell, Sluice, we ain't storekeepers. What do we want with a store?"

"Listen to me. There's a man name of Grimes what owns this whole damn town. I made a deal with him for this place. It'll give us a cover for hanging around till we can take over from him. You see?"

"Well, yeah, I think so. We going to take over the whole fucking town? The saloon?"

"That's right."

"It got gals?"

"Plenty of them. Good-looking ones, too."

"Jailhouse?"

"Hell, Jigs, you can be the sheriff if you want to."

"I can wear a badge?"

"You damn right."

"Hey, Sluice, I had you all wrong. I'm sorry, pard."

"Forget it, Jigs," said Sluice. "Come on with me now over to the saloon and we'll have a few drinks. You can meet Grimes, too, but don't let on that anything's wrong. Okay?"

"I won't let on nothing," said Jigs. "You can count on me for that."

Billy Pierce rode into North Fork and found Old Jan in the saloon. He had one drink with his old partner, and then Old Jan took him to the doctor's office to see Slocum. Slocum was sitting up in bed when they walked in. "He's coming along pretty well," said Doc. "He'll be getting up in another few days, I imagine."

"Slocum," said Billy, "I'm glad to see you coming along so good."

"Where's Gourd?" Slocum asked.

"He's buried over in Jones Mill," said Billy. "They got him on the road. Ambush. Not before we got one of them, though."

"Which one?" said Slocum, his voice anxious.

"Not Sluice," said Billy. "Sluice and one other one are still out there somewhere."

"What do you intend to do now, Billy boy?" said Old Jan.

Billy shrugged. "Hang around here with you two, I guess," he said.

"Jan," said Slocum.

"Yeah?"

"Why don't you leave Billy here, like he said, and you go on ahead. Have those two ever laid eyes on you?"

"I don't believe they have," said Old Jan.

"Well, you ride on ahead. See if you can locate them. Hang back and keep your eyes on them. That way, when I come along, me and Billy, you can show us where they're at."

"Well," said Old Jan, "I guess I could do that."

"Here," said Billy, "you might need some of this."

He pulled a wad of bills out of his pocket and handed them to Old Jan.

"Where the hell did you get all that?" said Old Jan.

"Charlie got it off the man we killed. I got it off Charlie."

Old Jan stuffed the money into his pocket. "I'll move out first thing in the morning, Slocum."

"They went past Jones Mill," said Billy. "Headed for Kansas, I think."

"Okay," said Old Jan. "I'll find them all right."

"Don't try to take them by yourself," said Slocum. "Just keep them in sight and wait for us."

"Don't worry about that," Old Jan said. "I'll be watching for you."

"The sheriff over in Jones Mill sent out the word on them," said Billy. "At least, he told me he was going to do that."

"I don't care about that," said Slocum. "I don't want anyone else getting to them before I do."

"Well then," said Old Jan, "you better get yourself well. You better get yourself up and around right away. The way that fool Sluice operates, someone's going to get pissed off at him and shoot him in the back pretty damn soon."

"If that happens," said Slocum, "I want you to know about it."

"I will."

"Right now," said Slocum, "I want one of you boys to go buy a bottle of good whiskey and bring it over here. And watch out for that doc when you do. He's kind of small-minded about things like that."

8

Sluice and Jigs had worked the store for about a week and had piled up some money in the cash drawer. Sluice gave Jigs enough money to keep him satisfied, but Jigs was getting impatient for some action. He was not cut out to be a storekeeper. He was standing behind the counter when a tough-looking man wearing two guns and badly needing a shave came walking in and up to the counter.

"What do you want?" said Jigs.

"I've come to collect for Mr. Grimes," the man said.

"Collect?" said Jigs. "Collect for what?"

"Grimes's cut," the man said.

"Cut of what?"

"Now listen, stupid," the man said. "Grimes gets a percentage of everything that's made in here. Maybe your boss forgot to tell you, so I'll forgive your fucking attitude for now. Where's your boss?"

"You mean Sl—uh, Mr. Callendar?"

"Sure I mean Callendar. Where the hell is he?"

"I believe he's in the back room taking a nap," said Jigs, "and he don't like to be disturbed when he's taking a nap."

"Well, this is damned important, little shit," said the man. "You go fetch him out here or I'll do it my own self."

"Don't you touch nothing while I'm out of the room," Jigs said. He walked through the door to the back room, and found Sluice sitting at the desk and doing some figuring in a ledger book.

"Hey, Sluice," he said, "there's some yokel out there saying he's come to collect for Grimes."

"Oh, yeah?" said Sluice. "I been expecting him. Tell him I'll be right out."

"Okay," said Jigs, and he walked back into the main room. The collection man was sucking on a piece of candy he had taken out of the jar on the counter. "Hey," Jigs said, "I told you to keep your hands off of things. You owe me a penny for that candy."

"Fuck you," said the man. "Where's your boss?"

"He's coming," said Jigs.

The back door opened, and Sluice stepped out holding a shotgun leveled at the man.

"You want me?" Sluice said.

"Put down that goddamn scattergun," the man said. "I'm here from Grimes for his dough."

"I'd say you come in here to rob me," said Sluice, and he pulled the trigger, blasting the man back against the wall. "Drag him out of here," he said to Jigs.

Jigs took hold of one of the man's legs and dragged him to the front door and out onto the sidewalk. Then he kicked the body out into the street. He walked back inside, stepping in the trail of blood he had left behind and leaving bloody boot prints where he walked thereafter.

"It's started," said Sluice.

Old Jan had made his way during the past week to Bascomb. He rode into the town and stopped at the saloon. Hitching his horse, he went inside. At the bar, Grimes asked him what he wanted. Old Jan ordered a shot of whiskey. Grimes gave it to him and took his money.

"You just passing through, mister?" he asked.

"That's right," said Old Jan.

"I'd advise you to hurry along your way then," Grimes

said. "This place is liable to turn into a bloody battlefield any time now."

"Really?" said Old Jan.

"Any time," said Grimes.

"Well, what's happening?"

"Man over at the general store calls himself Callendar just killed one of my employees. We're going after him soon as the rest of my men show up."

"Callendar, huh?" said Old Jan.

"That's the name he gave me," Grimes said.

"I reckon you're right, then," said Old Jan. "I best be on my way. Thanks for the drink and the advice."

"You bet," said Grimes.

Old Jan walked out the door, mounted up, and rode straight to the general store. He dismounted again, tied his horse again, and walked inside. He noticed the long stream of blood right away. He recognized Sluice from the murder trial. He did not think the two men knew him by sight. He hoped that he was right as he walked to the counter.

"You got some chawing tobacco?" he asked.

"Right there behind you, old-timer," said Jigs. "You blind?"

Old Jan turned and found the tobacco. He picked out what he wanted, turned back to the counter, and paid for it.

"Yeah," he said. "Sometimes I can't see anything if it's right under my own nose. Thanks now."

He got no response, so he just turned and walked back out onto the sidewalk, back down to his horse waiting at the hitching rail. He untied it, mounted up, and turned it north, riding back out of town. Once outside of Bascomb, he relaxed. He had been right. They did not know him. He turned west the first opportunity he found and sought the high ground. The higher the better. He needed a perch from which he could watch the road in both directions.

Grimes and two more of his men stepped out into the street together. Each man wore two six-guns and carried a shotgun. They stood for a moment on the sidewalk and stared toward the general store.

"They still in there?" asked one of the gunmen.

"I've had the place watched the whole time, Carter," said Grimes. "They're both in there all right."

"Should we wait for the others?" Carter asked.

"The three of us is plenty," said the other man. "We'll take them."

Carter looked at Grimes. "No," Grimes said. "We ain't waiting. Let's go get them right now."

They checked their weapons and started walking. Three abreast, they headed for the hardware store. Grimes said, "Spread out now," and they separated a bit. Inside the store, Sluice was looking out the window and saw them coming.

"Jigs," he said, "there's three of them coming. Get out the back door and circle around to the corner of the building there. I'll stay here."

"Gotcha, Sluice," Jigs said, and he hurried out the back door.

Out in the street, Grimes and the other two stopped short of the building. They stood for a moment looking at it. Grimes could see the outline of the man he knew as Callendar through the front window. Callendar was holding a rifle. "Callendar," Grimes shouted. "Callendar, can you hear me?"

"Sure, I hear you," Sluice answered.

"Our contract is void, you son of a bitch," Grimes yelled. "Come on out of there."

"You come in," Sluice called out. "Come on in. Someone'll have to carry you back out, though."

"Where's your little chickenshit pard?" said Grimes.

At the corner of the building, Jigs cranked a shell into the chamber of his rifle. "Right here," he hollered, "taking a bead on your chest."

"You're outnumbered," Grimes said.

"Not by much and not for long," said Sluice. He smashed the window with his rifle barrel, took a quick aim, and fired a shot at Grimes. It was too quick a shot, and it just tore a little flesh in Grimes's left arm.

"Ow. Shit," Grimes yelled, raising his own rifle to his shoulder and firing back through the window. Sluice ducked down low and the bullet flew harmlessly across the store, smashing a can of peaches on a shelf on the back wall.

At the corner of the building, Jigs took aim at Grimes, but a couple of horses at a hitch rail blocked Jigs's shot. He jockeyed around for a better one. Carter ducked low and fired a round at Jigs from under a horse's belly. The bullet nicked the side of the store building sending splinters flying into Jigs's face. He dropped his rifle.

"Yikes," he yelped. "Ow." His hands both flew to his face. Another shot hit too close for comfort, and Jigs, still covering his face with both hands, moved farther back down the wall, disappearing from the sight of Grimes and his men.

"Take cover," Grimes said. He ran toward the store and pressed himself against the front wall. Carter ran toward Jigs and did the same. He was leaning against the wall just around the corner from where Jigs was hiding. The third man ducked behind a watering trough that stood near the sidewalk in front of the store. He put his rifle down and pulled out a six-gun. He looked at the broken window, waiting and hoping that "Callendar" would show himself again. Soon, Sluice popped up again in the window looking for a target. He saw no one and ducked down again just as the man behind the trough fired a shot. It went right over Sluice's head and opened a hole in the pickle barrel, allowing a stream of pickle juice to spurt out onto the floor.

Jigs had finally stopped whimpering over his splintered face, picked up his rifle, and peeked around the corner of the building. He spotted the man behind the trough, took quick aim, and fired, dropping the man, but in doing so, he exposed himself to Carter, who fired a shot that took off the end of Jigs's nose. Jigs yelped again.

"Ow. Yow. Oh, Goddamn." He jumped back again. Carter was about to ease himself around the corner for a finishing shot, but just then, Sluice stepped out the front door and shot him in the back. Carter sprawled on his face dead. Behind Sluice, Grimes raised his rifle, but Sluice turned and fired another quick shot, just missing Grimes, and ran back into the store. Grimes was alone. He hesitated a moment, then turned and ran down the street. He made it safely back to the saloon and ran inside. Going back behind the bar, he poured himself a drink and downed it. He stood there breathing heavily. He had lost two of his best men. He should have waited for the others.

Sluice had seen Grimes go into the saloon from his place at the window. He knew that the other two had been killed. It was reasonably safe outside by then, so he stepped out and walked down to the corner of the building. Looking around the corner, he saw Jigs squatted down against the wall holding his face.

"Jigs," he said. "How bad you hit?"

"By doze," Jigs burbled. "Dey shot by doze."

"Here," said Sluice, "let me see."

He caught Jigs by the shirtfront and pulled him to his feet. Then he pulled Jigs's hands away from his face.

"Ooow," moaned Jigs.

"Goddamn," said Sluice. "You're a fucking mess." Jigs whined and whimpered. "Come on," said Sluice, taking him by an arm. "Let's get inside."

"By whole head hurds," said Jigs. "Id's esbloding."

"Come on." Sluice took him inside. He found a chair and made Jigs sit down. Then he looked around. The pickle barrel was still spurting juice. He grabbed a small pan from off a nearby shelf and held it in the stream until the pan was nearly full. Then he walked back over to where Jigs was sitting and crying, and tossed the juice into Jigs's face. Jigs screamed. He shrieked. Sluice tossed a towel in his face. Jigs held the towel in both his hands and daubed at his face gingerly.

"All right. All right," said Sluice. "Stop that howling and crying. I've had enough of it."

"You ain't neber had your doze shod off," said Jigs.

In the saloon, Grimes poured himself another drink. He was pissed off. He had a deal with Callendar, and he had been double-crossed in a big way. He had sent his man to collect his due share, and that bastard Callendar had murdered him.

Why had he done that? The only explanation Grimes could think of was that Callendar was deliberately trying to start a war with him. Callendar had been badly outnumbered originally. He had been one man against seven. Then his pal had showed up. It had been two to seven. Now they had killed three of Grimes's men, so it had come down to four against those two. The odds were improving for Callendar all the time. Grimes downed his drink and poured another. When his three other boys showed up, he would have to come up with a different plan. They would not just go over to the store again. That had been disastrous. Maybe he should get some more men in on this.

He picked up his third drink and sipped at it. A couple of cowhands came in and ordered beers. Grimes served them and took their money. He wished that his other three men would show up. Maybe they could help him figure out how to approach this situation, how to get that goddamned Callendar and his pal. He was curious about Callendar. Now that the man had started giving him so much trouble, he wondered where the son of a bitch had come from and who he was. He should have wondered that earlier, but it was too late to worry about that now. He had received quite a bunch of correspondence intended for the sheriff of Bascomb. Since Bascomb had no sheriff, and since Grimes owned it all, he got that mail and the wires and so on. He decided to look through it.

He went back to his office and pulled a stack of papers out of a desk drawer. The first several were unimportant. Then he came to the wire from the sheriff of Jones Mill, Wyoming. It described a killer named Sluice who was known to be traveling the road south and would likely come through the town. Sluice might be traveling with a companion called Jigs. The description of Sluice fit Callendar to a T. So Callendar was actually Sluice, Grimes thought. Callendar was Sluice. Goddamn it.

9

Slocum was up and walking around. He got up early in the morning and dressed. Billy Pierce came by for him, and they went out to breakfast together. They sat for a good long time and drank lots of coffee. Slocum was back in Doc's office after that until lunchtime, and then the two went out again for a meal. They back to the office again for the afternoon, and then out again for the evening meal. It should have been a pleasant enough recuperation, but Slocum was bored, he was disgusted, he was longing to get back on the road and get after Sluice and Jigs. He figured that Billy was feeling about the same, even though Billy was just waiting around for Slocum. Slocum hated to admit it, but he was tired out after each of his meals. He needed rest.

One morning after breakfast, he told Billy that he wanted to get his horse and take a ride. Billy noticed that Slocum was wearing his Colt that morning. He did not ask any questions, though. Instead, he walked to the stable with Slocum and they saddled their horses. They rode a ways out of town and stopped alongside a creek that was running there. Slocum found some small rocks and set them up in a row. When Billy figured out what Slocum was up to, he helped him. Soon, they had a long row of rocks. They walked back a distance, and Slocum pulled his Colt as fast as he could and fired. It was not very fast, and he missed his target. He cursed under his breath and tried again. He hit the rock, but he was slow.

Billy had been inactive for a time, too, so he tried his hand. He was better than Slocum, and Slocum knew that he should not be. The wound and the inactivity had sure slowed him down. He hated it. He cursed himself yet again for having let himself get ambushed that way. Suckered like a goddamned kid. A greenhorn. He kept shooting, and mostly he hit his targets, but mostly remained slow, and he was hurting his side and his chest. At last, he told Billy that he was ready to go back to town. It was lunchtime by the time they got back. When he made it back to Doc's office, Nurse McGee was almost furious with him.

"Where have you been?" she demanded.

"Aw, I had breakfast with Billy, and we decided to go out for a little ride," he said. "That's all. Well, we had lunch when we got back."

"You should let us know when you're going to be out that long," Jill said.

"Sorry," said Slocum.

"Let me see your gun," she said.

"What?"

"You heard me," she said. "Let me see it."

"You going to shoot me?" Slocum asked.

She did not respond. She just looked at him with disgust and held out her hand. Slocum pulled out the Colt, turned it around to hand it to her butt-first, and she took it. She held it up to her nose and sniffed it. She handed it back to him, and he holstered it.

"You've been out shooting," she said.

"Just target practice," he said.

"Well, I think you should get back in bed," she said. "Right now."

"I think you're right," Slocum said. "I'm tired."

"I should think so."

Slocum went into the other room and took off his hat and his gun belt. Then he sat down on the edge of the bed and pulled off his boots. He picked up his feet and put them on the bed, stretching himself out with a groan. Jill scowled at him. Just then, Billy Pierce stepped into the room.

"I put the horses up," he said.

"Thanks, Billy," Slocum said.

Jill turned angrily on Billy. "Did you take him out shooting this morning?" she demanded.

"Well, I—"

"I went out shooting," said Slocum. "Billy just rode along with me. That's all."

She turned angrily and stalked away, going about her work, or just doing her best to look busy. Doc Harman came in then. He said howdy to Billy and then opened Slocum's shirt to change the bandage and check the wound. Jill came back to the bedside to stand by in case she was needed.

"It's looking good," said Doc. "You'll be up and around in just a few days."

"He was up and around already today," Jill said, still huffy. "He was out shooting all morning."

"Is that right?" Doc said. "How'd you do?"

"Not so well," said Slocum. "I've been laid up too long, I guess."

"Well, you'll get better again," said Doc. "You'll live to kill again, I reckon."

"I will," said Slocum.

"I'm going to release you," Doc said. "No need for you to hang around in here any longer. Just take it easy for a few days yet. Don't do anything too strenuous. Come in and see me in the afternoons. You'll be out on your own pretty damn soon now."

"Thanks, Doc," Slocum said.

Slocum moved into the hotel room that Billy was staying in. It was the same one that Old Jan had first occupied. The next few days were routine. They would get up and have breakfast, ride out for a morning of shooting practice, ride back in for lunch, hang around town in the afternoon, have supper, have a few drinks, then go to bed. One night when they had been drinking for a little while, Billy Pierce was feeling a bit woozy.

"Slocum," he said, "I'm going up to the room."

"Had a bit much, have you?" said Slocum. "Well, go on. I'll be along in a little bit."

Slocum had a couple more drinks, then decided that maybe Billy had been right. He left the saloon, and was heading down the street when he heard his name called. He looked around.

"Over here," came the voice. "Across the street."

He recognized the voice of Jill McGee. Looking across the street, he saw her standing in front of her house. He turned and walked over to see her and find out why she had called to him. Approaching her in her yard, he took off his hat.

"Good evening, Nurse McGee," he said.

"Mr. Slocum," she said, "you're out late."

"Just a little," he said. "You're still up, I see."

Ignoring his remark, she said, "How are you feeling?"

"I feel pretty good," he said. "I figure I'll be leaving here tomorrow morning."

"On the killing trail?" she said.

"Nurse McGee—"

"Why don't you call me Jill?" she asked.

"All right, Jill," he said.

"What can I call you?"

"Slocum's just fine."

"All right, Slocum. Would you like to come in for a drink?"

He gestured toward her front door. "In—in there?" he said. "Your house?"

"I won't be seen in a saloon," she said.

"No. Of course not."

"Well?"

"Yes, ma'am—Jill. I sure would."

She led the way into the house and gestured toward a seat on the couch. He sat down, tossing his hat onto a table.

Jill was pouring a couple of drinks across the room. She glanced over her shoulder.

"You don't need to keep wearing that gun in here," she said.

Slocum stood up and unbuckled his belt. He laid it on the table beside his hat. And sat back down. Jill walked over and handed him a drink. Then she sat down beside him and held up her glass. Slocum touched his glass to it, and they drank.

Over in his hotel room, Billy Pierce was thinking about Slocum. He was also thinking about Old Jan and about Sluice. He hoped that Old Jan was all right, that he was doing what Slocum had told him to do, keeping his eyes on Sluice and Jigs but keeping himself out of sight. Billy was sick of losing his friends, first Trent Brady, then Charlie Gourd. Slocum had come awful close, too damn close, and Billy sure did not want anything bad to happen to Old Jan. He knew how Slocum felt about getting Sluice himself, but secretly he hoped that when they caught up with Sluice, he would already be dead. Billy could not walk out on Slocum, and he could not walk away from the hunt for Sluice, but he did want this all to be over with. He had an idea that Slocum was about ready to hit the road again. His shooting had improved much in the last few days. Well, Billy was nervous about resuming the chase, but he was ready just the same.

Old Jan did not know exactly what had happened down in the town of Bascomb, but he knew there had been some shooting. He was pretty sure that Sluice and Jigs were both holed up in the general store. For some reason, Sluice had gotten himself crossways with someone else in the town. Old Jan thought that it was that Grimes from the saloon. A couple of men had been killed, but he was pretty sure that Sluice and Jigs were alive and well, and he knew damn well that Slocum would be after them soon. He thought about going back to North Fork and telling Slocum that they were safe and sound and appeared to be settled in at Bascomb for a spell, but then, he had promised that he would stick with Sluice and Jigs. And who knew what would happen? They might slicker out of Bascomb at any moment. They might get their asses killed at any moment. No, Old Jan figured, he had better stay put right where he was. He'd better keep his eyes on the situation.

Slocum was stripped naked in Jill's bedroom, and he helped slicker her out of the last of her garments. She turned naked toward the bed and threw the covers down completely. Then she crawled in on her hands and knees, displaying her ample butt to Slocum as she did so. He admired it as she moved, and then he crawled in behind her. She rolled over onto her back and spread her legs, and Slocum moved right on top of her. He let his weight down on her, and kissed her fully on the lips. She responded delightfully, her arms wrapping around his back and pulling him tight and close. Then she slid her hands down his back to his butt, and she squeezed the cheeks hard. Slocum humped downward. She let her hands move underneath him and feel for his cock and balls. The cock was hard and ready for action. She squeezed it in one fist and felt it buck and throb. Her other hand moved underneath his balls, and she held them in her palm as if weighing them.

"Are you ready to go?" she asked him.

"I've never been more ready," he said.

She moved the head of his rod to her waiting slit and rubbed it up and down. Her waiting cunt was slippery, wet, and juicy. At last, she guided the head into her waiting hole, and Slocum thrust, driving his tool deep into her cavern.

"Ahh," she moaned.

His entire length was inside her. She raised her pelvis, grinding it against his, writhing herself against him. Slowly, Slocum withdrew until all of his cock but the head was out. Then he shoved it back in, still slowly, again all the way. He did this again and again. Jill was getting anxious for him to drive harder and faster. She dug her nails into his butt and humped hard against him. Then, at last, Slocum drove into her hard. He started pumping hard and fast, and she matched her movements to his. Their bodies slapped together loudly. Slap. Slap, slap.

"Oh, oh, oh," she moaned.

"Ahh," said Slocum, almost growling.

"Give it to me," she said. "Give it to me hard. Harder."

Slocum suddenly and unexpectedly withdrew his rod completely.

"Oh?" she said.

He grabbed her by the waist with both hands and turned her over, pulling her up onto her knees. Again, he had a view of that marvelous ass. He grasped his rod and found her hungry hole once again, and once again, he drove it in deep. Once again, she responded, shoving her ass hard against her crotch and belly. He slapped against her again and again. From his vantage point, he could see her pendulous tits bouncing as their bodies smacked together over and over. Slocum felt like he did not have much more in him, and he did not want to leave Jill unsatisfied. He pulled out again and lay down on his back, pulling Jill over on top of him.

She straddled him as if she were mounting a horse and eased herself down on his cock, taking in the whole length as she slid. He took her by the waist again. She began a slow rocking back and forth, sliding easily on his belly. Then she moved faster and faster, driving him to a near frenzy. He moved his hands up to her tits, grabbing one in each hand and rubbing her nipples with his thumbs. They stood out large and hardened.

Jill wore herself out and fell forward, her left breast touching Slocum's face. He took the nipple in his mouth and sucked hard. She pulled it out and moved the right one in. In a couple of minutes, she scooted backward just a bit, enough to allow their lips to come together. They kissed hard, parting their lips enough to allow their tongues to duel, to search around inside their mouths. Finally, Jill pulled away and sat up again. She started rocking again. Slocum felt his balls grow ready to explode. Before they did that, though, Jill began to groan low and long. She rocked harder and faster, and at last she stopped.

"Oh," she cried. "Oh, God. Oh, God, Slocum, that's enough. That did it. Oh, damn, damn, damn."

Slocum was about to drive some more in order to get himself off. It wouldn't take much. But before he could move, Jill had pulled herself off him. She wriggled back between his legs until her face was just above his desperate cock. Quickly, she slurped it into her mouth, and Slocum gasped out loud, sounding as if he had been hurt. Jill began bouncing her head up and down, slurping all the way. Slocum humped into her face. At last, the dam burst. He gushed forth into her mouth, and she swallowed each burst. When at last he had stopped, Jill got up and put on a gown. With her back to Slocum, she said, "I think you had better leave now."

Slocum sat up with a surprised look on his face. He was so stunned by her abruptness that he did not respond.

"I expect you'll be riding out of town soon," she said. "Perhaps even in the morning. I see no reason to prolong this. Good night."

She went into the next room, leaving Slocum alone to get dressed and get out of her house.

In the morning, Slocum and Billy had their breakfast as usual, except that they had their bedrolls along with them. They had checked out of the hotel. Finished with their meal, they left the eating place and headed for the livery stable. As they passed by the doctor's office, they saw Nurse Jill McGee going to work. She gave a curt nod. Slocum and Billy each touched the brims of their hats. No one said anything, and they walked on. At the stable, they paid the man, saddled their mounts, and climbed into their saddles. They rode out of town headed south. They were a few miles out before either man spoke a word.

"Slocum," said Billy Pierce. "I wonder how far south they got."

"We'll know that when we catch up with them," Slocum said.

"Yeah. I reckon Old Jan will see us coming first, and he'll come out to meet us. Tell us what's going on."

"I reckon."

In Bascomb, Grimes was in the saloon with his other men. He was planning an all-out assault on the general store. He had determined already that he was not going to make the same mistake as before. He was going to use fire this time. He was either going to burn them out or burn them up. Either way, he did not give a damn.

10

From his vantage point on the hill just outside of town, Old Jan watched as several men gathered at the saloon. What he could not know was that Sluice was also watching through the front window of the general store. Old Jan did not know that Sluice was surprised at the size of his opposition and that he decided to bail out while he had the chance. He did not hear Sluice tell Jigs to stay busy behind the counter while he checked something in the back room, adding that he did not think they would have any trouble from Grimes that day. Old Jan could not see Sluice slip out the back door and make his skulking way to the livery stable. He did see the gang gathering outside the saloon with Grimes at the forefront. He knew that something was about to happen, and he watched carefully.

The gang walked toward the general store, and Grimes stepped out in front. He stopped within shouting distance and called out. "Callendar, you cheap son of a bitch. Step out here like a man, and let's have a talk." He received no response. Inside the store, Jigs heard him shout. Sluice was wrong, he thought. Grimes is out there wanting to start something. He grabbed a rifle and checked its load. Then he rushed to the front window.

"Goddamn," he said, taking note of the size of the force

he was facing. Then he called out, "Sluice. They're out there. A whole fucking bunch of them." He waited a couple of minutes, and when he did not get an answer back, he called again. "Sluice." There was still no answer. "Hey," he called out to Grimes. "Hey out there. Give me a couple of minutes. I got to get Sluice."

"Sluice?" said Grimes. "You mean Callendar?"

"Yeah," said Jigs. "That's right. Callendar."

So, thought Grimes, Sluice is Callendar, or rather Callendar is Sluice. Just as I thought. He turned to his gang and motioned some of them around the house to watch the back. As they moved out, he called out again. "Where is Sluice?"

"He's in the back room," Jigs yelled. "It'll just take me a minute to get him out here."

"You've got a minute," said Grimes.

Down at the far end of the street, Sluice rode his horse out the back door of the stable and headed out of town. No one saw him go. No one in town. From his spot on the hilltop, Old Jan saw him go. He was headed south.

Jigs looked in the back room and found it deserted. He opened the back door and saw the members of Grimes's outfit out there looking mean as hell. He quickly shut the door and bolted it. He stood for a moment confused. Sluice had done it again. He had deserted him. Goddamn it, Jigs thought, and me with my fucking nose shot off, too. He went back into the main room and back to the front window. He looked out. Grimes was still standing there in front of his gang. Jigs went to the front door and opened it a crack, careful to stand to one side.

"Grimes," he called out.

"I'm here," said Grimes.

"Grimes, I, uh, Sluice ain't here."

"What the hell are you talking about?"

"I just looked in the back room, and he ain't there."

"What are you trying to pull on me?" Grimes said.

"He's run out on me," said Jigs, his voice trembling with rage at Sluice and with fear at the Grimes bunch. "The son of a bitch has run out on me again."

"You expect me to believe that shit?"

"If you'll promise not to kill me," said Jigs, "I'll toss my guns out, and you can come in here and look around."

Grimes turned to one of his men and said, "Run down to the livery stable and see if that goddamned bastard has got his horse and left."

"Right away, Boss," said the man, and he trotted off down the street.

"All right," said Grimes, raising his voice again. "Toss out your guns."

"You promise you won't kill me?" begged Jigs.

"You have my word," said Grimes.

Jigs swung the door wider open. He stepped back again and pressed himself against the wall. He waited. Nothing happened. He reached out and tossed the rifle out. Still nothing. He pulled out his six-gun and tossed it out. Then he stepped into the doorway with his hands held high. "Don't shoot," he said.

"You got my word," said Grimes. "Come on out."

Jigs stepped uneasily out onto the sidewalk, and Grimes motioned him forward. He stepped on wobbly legs out into the street and on up close to Grimes. Grimes punched him hard on the jaw, knocking him flat in the street.

"You give me your word," said Jigs.

"I haven't killed you, you little chickenshit," said Grimes.

Just then, the man who had gone to the stable returned. Coming up beside Grimes, he said, "He's gone, Boss. He got his horse a while ago. Probably before we come out here. He rode out the back way heading south, according to the liveryman."

"The son of a bitch," whimpered Jigs, still lying in the street. "I knowed that he had run out on me. Left me here all by my lone self to face the whole bunch of you. Never said a damn word. If ever I see him again, I'll kill the dirty bastard. I'll blow his fucking head off with a shotgun. I'll—"

"Shut up," said Grimes. "You'll have to get in line. Well, at least we're rid of him here in town."

"Can—can I go now?" Jigs sniveled. "You won't never see

me again. I promise you that. I'm just going to hunt down that goddamned Sluice. That's all."

"Stand up," said Grimes.

Jigs managed to get to his feet despite his weak legs. "I'll just pick up my guns and then go get my horse, and I'll be traveling on then. Thank you, Mr. Grimes. I'm sorry for any trouble I maybe caused you, but it really wasn't me. It was Sluice. I hope you realize that."

"Hold it right there," said Grimes.

"What?"

"Circle around him, boys," Grimes said.

"What?" said Jigs. "What is this?"

The gang moved in around Jigs. He backed up until he realized he was completely encircled. "You—you promised me," he said.

"All right, boys," said Grimes. "You heard him. I made him a promise. He's not to be killed. Remember that. Just give him something to remember us by—for a long time."

"No," said Jigs. "That ain't fair. You said you'd let me go. You said—"

"All I said was that I wouldn't kill you, you little weaselly son of a bitch. Have at him, boys."

One man reached out with a foot and kicked Jigs's legs viciously out from under him. Jigs fell hard on his back. He felt like a couple of ribs might have been broken. For sure, all his breath was knocked out of his lungs. He tried to suck hard to get some wind back, but he could not get his wind, and the sucking hurt his ribs. Another man reached down with both hands, grabbing him by the shirtfront and hauling him back up to his feet. Standing him up, the man drove a fist hard into Jigs's gut. Jigs doubled over. He felt as if he would die. He was not breathing. He could not get a breath. He knew that his head had turned blue. His legs had no strength. He would have fallen, but someone was holding him up. Whoever it was straightened him up again. He tried to talk. He wanted to tell them that they were killing him, and they were not supposed to do that.

He wondered how long he could live without catching a breath.

Grimes pulled one man out of the circle and sent him to the livery stable to fetch Jigs's horse and bring it to them. The man hurried off. The circle closed up a bit. A man struck Jigs in the face, hitting his already injured nose. Jigs tried to scream with the pain, but he could not. He did not have enough air in his lungs to manage a scream. He staggered back, falling into the arms of two other men. They grabbed his arms and held them tight, keeping Jigs on his feet. A man pounded him several times in the gut, and another stepped up to punch him in the face a few times. The men who were holding him up let him fall.

He was on his hands and knees, and someone kicked him hard in the ribs. He fell flat, and two or three men kicked him over and over again. At last, he sucked in some air. He was not at all sure what allowed him to do that, but he did not care. He was grateful. That was all. He sucked in more and more, and then, suddenly, they stopped kicking him. He lay there on his face in the dirt sucking in air.

"All right," Grimes said. "Pick him up and put him in the saddle."

He felt himself being pulled to his feet again, and then he felt himself being tossed through the air. He was sitting in a saddle. Hands turned him loose. He sat uneasily for a moment, and then he fell, landing hard again on the ground.

"Put him back," said Grimes, "and this time, tie him to the saddle."

He was picked up one more time, tossed again into the saddle, and then, with hands holding him in place, other hands wrapped a rope around him. He felt the rope being pulled tight. They turned loose of him, and he tried to fall again, but he could not. The rope was holding him in place. Then someone slapped the horse on the rump, and it took off. Jigs felt himself jerk back, but he did not fall. He would have fallen had he not been tied down. The horse raced off with him, heading south out of town.

From his place on the hill, Old Jan watched it all. His

assignment had been to keep an eye on Sluice and Jigs. He got up and saddled his horse. He started down the hill and headed south on the road. Sluice was out there somewhere. Old Jan had no idea how far ahead he had gotten. Jigs was not far. He had to follow them, but his immediate problem was getting through Bascomb. Things were pretty tense down there just then, and he was not at all certain that he could ride through the town unmolested. But he would have to try. He could not see that he had any choice.

Down on the road, he headed into Bascomb. He rode slow and easy. Soon, he was moving into the town. He was pleased to see that the gang had moved out of the street and into the saloon. Even so, he still did not think that he could move through without detection. He kept going. He was riding past the saloon when Grimes stepped out.

"Hey, you," Grimes called out.

Old Jan stopped his horse and looked over toward Grimes.

"You mean me?" he asked.

"Yeah, you," said Grimes. "I've seen you in here before, ain't I?"

"That's right," Old Jan answered.

"Where you going?"

"Just passing through," said Old Jan.

"Come on over here," said Grimes.

Old Jan turned his horse and rode slowly over to where Grimes stood on the sidewalk in front of the saloon. He stopped his horse there.

"What's your business, mister?" said Grimes. "Why are you riding back and forth like this?"

Old Jan thought quickly. He decided that the best thing was probably to just tell the truth.

"I've got two partners back in North Fork," he said. "We set out together, with one more man, tracking the men that killed our friend and our boss. We got one of them, but they killed one of us and wounded another. Hurt him pretty bad. Him and the other one are back at North Fork waiting for the wound to heal up. They sent me on to keep my eyes on the prey. Two men. Sluice and Jigs. My partners will be following me before long. I can't lose those two I'm watching."

"Sluice and Jigs, huh?" said Grimes. "I want that damned Sluice myself. I guess I'll just wish you luck for now. Ride on."

Old Jan touched the brim of his hat and moved out, heaving a sigh of relief.

Up ahead on the road, Jigs bounced along painfully. At last, he had air in his lungs again, but it was still agony to breathe because of his stove-in ribs, so his breaths were shallow. His injured nose caused his entire face, even his whole head, to throb with pain. His vision was still blurred, and everything in his eyesight had a slight red tinge to it. He felt like cursing everyone, Sluice, Grimes, those men who were chasing them, the whole fucking world, but he didn't have the energy. He rode along, his head bobbing on his shoulders. His hands were free, and he thought that he could untie himself, but then, he considered that he probably still could use the stability the ropes gave him. At last, he came to a stream running alongside the road, and he stopped. He managed to get the rope untied, and he slipped from the saddle. His legs collapsed under the weight of his body when his feet hit the ground. It took him some time, but at last he managed to get the horse unsaddled and picketed near the stream. He stretched himself out nearby. Soon he was asleep.

When Old Jan came riding by, he did not notice where Jigs had moved off the road. He went right past the sleeping man, still in pursuit of Sluice. As he rode along, he wondered how far behind him Slocum and Billy Pierce were. He wondered if Slocum was yet able to ride and to shoot. The shooting was important. Slocum would need his shooting arm when he caught up with Sluice—if they ever caught up with the no-good bastard. The sun was already dropping low in the western sky, and Old Jan knew that he would have to stop somewhere sometime soon for the night. He started watching for a good place to make a camp.

Sluice was riding hard. He knew that night was falling, but he was anxious to get lots of room between him and anyone who might be following. He figured that Grimes and his men had already killed Jigs. They'd had plenty of time to accomplish that task. They might be in pursuit of Sluice now. He rode hard, knowing that he was killing his horse. He just hoped that he would come across another one in time to make a trade. Then he would keep riding hard. He would ride well into the night. He would leave his pursuers far behind. He was also hoping to come across a road that would lead him either east or west, or better yet, a road that would lead east and west, thus giving him a chance to confuse his pursuers. He had plenty of cash on him, but it would not last him forever. He had to find a place where he could settle down for a spell and make even more.

He cursed himself for being a fool back in Bascomb and making his move against Grimes way too soon. He'd had no idea how many men Grimes had at his call, though. He had been surprised by that. He should have waited longer. He'd had a nice setup there. Damn it all to hell. Well, he could get another one somewhere else. He would.

Slocum and Billy rode along slowly. They did not talk much, but both men were anxious to come across Old Jan, knowing that he would have Sluice and Jigs spotted and would be keeping track of them.

"Slocum," said Billy, "don't you think we'll have to stop before long? It'll be getting dark."

"We'll keep going for a while, Billy," Slocum said. "We'll make it a short night."

"The road is good along here," Billy said. "As long as we ride easy, we shouldn't have no problems."

"Yeah."

"Slocum?"

"What?"

"You got yourself ambushed once. Charlie was ambushed and killed. We sure will have to be careful. We don't want that to happen again."

"We'll be careful, Billy. Don't worry about that. And this time, we have Old Jan watching things for us. We ought to be just fine, at least until we come across Old Jan."

11

Sluice was moving much more slowly. He had ridden all through the night. Soon, it would be daylight again. His tired horse was about to drop under him. He had ridden it near to death. He knew that he could not go much farther on it, and he sure as hell did not want to be walking out in the middle of nowhere. Had he paced his horse better, he would still have a good mount, but he did not consider that. He considered only that he was almost surely being pursued, and he intended to get away safely. So far in his life, he had learned, or so he thought, that everything always worked out in his favor, no matter how bleak things might appear to be at first.

And then he saw the lane turning off to the left. It had to go somewhere. He turned the horse down the lane, and had not ridden long before he saw a small house, a thin plume of smoke rising from the chimney. If there was a house and a fire, there had to be a horse. He stopped at a distance from the house where his horse would not be heard, then dismounted, pulled out his six-gun, and started walking toward the house. When he got a little closer, he saw the small corral behind the house. He moved cautiously toward it. There were two horses, pretty good-looking ones at that. Then a dog started barking.

"Goddamn," he said, jumping with fright. Cursing himself

for having been so easily frightened, he looked around. The dog was standing at one corner of the house growling and barking. If there was anyone at home, the dog would have roused him by this time. A shot wouldn't matter a bit. Sluice aimed the six-gun and fired. The dog yelped and jerked and fell dead. The front door of the house flew open, and a man with a shotgun in his hands stepped out looking around wildly.

"Max," he said. "Where are you?"

His answer was a shot from Sluice's revolver. The bullet slammed into his chest, knocking him over backward onto the floor just inside his door. He kicked once and then lay still. Sluice hurried over to look at his bloody work. The man was dead. Sluice stepped over the body quickly, gun held ready, and looked around the room. It was empty. The man was alone. Sluice relaxed. He had all kinds of time. He had two good horses outside, and he had a house to himself. There would be food. He started to rummage around, and he found a bottle of whiskey. He pulled out the cork and had a swig. Then he continued looking for something to eat.

Old Jan had stopped but a few hours for the night. He had roused himself early and resumed his journey while it was still dark. He moved along the road slowly. For one thing, he wanted to spare his horse. For another, he did not want to come across Sluice by surprise, either his surprise or Sluice's. The road along which he traveled was hard-packed and rocky, and he could detect no telltale tracks. He only knew that Sluice had moved out in this direction. When he came to the narrow lane that turned off to the left, he paused. He could not tell if anyone had ridden down that way. He hesitated. Sluice had left Bascomb in a hurry. Old Jan could think of no reason for Sluice to slow his escape to turn down a narrow lane along the way. No reason, except—with the pace he had been setting, Sluice would have ruined his horse. He might wonder if there would be a horse available down the lane. Old Jan decided to take a chance on letting Sluice get farther away from him by spending a little time to check out this lane. He turned his horse and started riding to the left.

The early morning sun was beginning to light the eastern horizon. Grimes left a few men to run his essential businesses, particularly the saloon, and mounted up with the rest of them to pursue Sluice. He made his men pack plenty of provisions for the trail. He did not want to have to stop his pursuit because of lack of supplies. There were nine men riding with Grimes, making a total of ten, and each man was heavily armed with a rifle and at least two revolvers. They rode out of Bascomb, making noise like a small army, with the pounding of horses' hoofs, the creaking of saddle leather, and the clattering of arms. Grimes rode in the lead like a commanding general. Their faces were all hard-set and grim.

Sluice finished his meal and drank down some more of his latest victim's whiskey. The bottle was empty, and he threw it across the room. He packed up some food that he could carry along the trail, and then he went outside. He fetched his nearly ruined horse and led it to the corral. There he switched its saddle to a fresh horse. Throwing a rope around the neck of the other fresh horse, he tied the one end of the rope to his saddle horn. Next time he wore out a horse, he would have his spare right at hand. He mounted up and started back toward the road leading the spare mount.

Just as he rounded a curve in the lane, he came face-to-face with Old Jan. Surprised, he jerked out his revolver and fired. His horse reared in fright at the sudden noise, as did the spare he led and Old Jan's horse. The bullet missed Old Jan, but his spooked horse tossed him off to the side of the road. Old Jan rolled quickly out of sight into the thick bramble that grew there. He scrambled to his hands and knees and crawled deeper into the thicket.

Sluice finally got control of his horse and dismounted. He started into the thicket, but after only a few steps, he stopped.

He looked into the thicket, but he could not see clearly. The sun was still low in the sky, and the thicket was not well lighted. He could not see the man he had shot at. If the man was armed, he could be lying in ambush. He could have a bead on Sluice already, waiting for him to step closer, waiting for the perfect shot.

"Fuck him," Sluice said, and he backed out of the tangle, back out onto the road. He remounted and started to ride again, but he grabbed the reins of Old Jan's horse as he passed it by. Now he had three horses. That was good, but what was even better was that the other man had none. He kicked his mount in the sides to hurry away from possible danger. Soon, he was back out on the main road heading south again. His belly was full of not particularly good food and cheap whiskey.

Old Jan waited a safe time before poking his head out again. The lane was clear. There was no sign of Sluice or of any of the three horses. Old Jan knew that he would have to walk now. He heaved a heavy sigh and walked out onto the lane. He started to follow Sluice, but decided that he should walk on down the lane first. He saw the house soon, and as soon as he saw it, he could see the feet of the body sticking out through the front door.

"Oh, hell," he said.

He walked on, and then he saw the corral and Sluice's played-out horse standing nearby. The living took precedence over the dead, even if it was a horse. He found some oats near the corral and poured some out in a trough for the spent animal. He made sure there was water, and he led the horse into the corral. Then he walked to the front door of the house. He stepped over the body into the house, and he could see that it had been ransacked. He was somewhat pleased to find out that there was but one victim. He looked around some more until he found a shovel, and then he went outside and dug a grave. He put the body in the hole and covered it up. Then he went back to the corral. He found a saddle, blanket, and harness, and he got the tired horse ready to ride, but he did not climb on its back. It was not ready for that. He started walking back toward the road, leading the horse.

Jigs woke up in his spot there beside the stream. The first thing he noticed was that he hurt all over. There was no place on his wretched body that was not throbbing with pain. His first effort to sit up was not successful. It accomplished nothing but sending sharper pains throughout his body. He groaned out loud and lay back again whimpering. "Goddamn that fucking Sluice," he said out loud. "And double damn that son of a bitch Grimes." The effort hurt him, so he shut up. He knew that he would have to try again to get up. He could not just lie there until he died. And he knew that it would take longer to heal up than it would to die. He tried again, but it hurt worse. He lay back and cried for a spell.

With a supreme effort, he rolled over onto his stomach. The agony was so great that he screamed out loud, but he made it. He lay there for a spell taking shallow breaths. Even those hurt his ribs. At last, he pulled his knees up under him, and he pushed himself up on his hands. Every move hurt. Finally, he stood up. His legs were wobbly, but he managed to walk to the edge of the stream, and there beside his horse, he dropped back down on his belly and dipped his swollen and bloody head into the water. He drank. The swallowing hurt him. He soaked his head. At last, he managed to get himself up into a sitting position again.

"How long?" he cried. "How long will it take?"

He sat there feeling sorry for himself and assessing his situation. He was hurt so bad he could hardly move. It even hurt him to breathe. He had no food and no weapons. There might be people after him. If he started to move again, he might come across Sluice. Any way he turned, it seemed to him, was certain death. He had to think of something. He wanted to survive. He wanted revenge. He wanted it on Sluice, and he wanted it on Grimes. He remembered that he had money. He had plenty of money. But it was not doing him any good here and now. He would have to get himself to civilization somehow. Then he could use it. He could buy food and whiskey and guns and ammunition. He could get a room with a soft bed and lay up in it until he was healed.

He heard the sound of horses moving down the road, and as badly as it hurt, he crawled closer to the road and hid himself behind a tree to watch. They came closer, and he recognized Grimes and his men, the same men who had tortured him and hurt him so badly. He fervently wished that he had some weapons. He wanted desperately to kill them. But even more desperately, he did not want them to kill him. Letting him live one time might have used up all the charity they had in them. He hugged the tree until they were gone. Riding on. Riding after Sluice, he expected.

It was around noon when Slocum and Billy Pierce rode into Bascomb. Slocum was sagging a bit in his saddle. Billy said, "There's a saloon, Slocum. You need to stop for a bit?"

"It wouldn't hurt, I reckon," Slocum said.

They pulled up in front of the saloon, tied their horses, and went inside. The place was almost deserted, but there was a barkeep behind the bar and a couple of farmers sitting at one table. Slocum and Billy walked to the bar.

"Bottle of whiskey," said Slocum. "Two glasses."

"Coming right up," said the barkeep.

He placed the order on the bar in front of them and poured out two drinks. Slocum paid him.

"Thanks," the barkeep said.

"Say," said Slocum. "What's going on around here? The town seems almost deserted."

"Yeah." said the barkeep. "Well, it is damn near. We had a little action here, and then Mr. Grimes, he's the boss around here, he took off with a bunch of men after a damned killer."

"Oh, yeah?" said Slocum.

"We're on the trail of a damned killer," said Billy Pierce.

"He got a name?" asked the barkeep.

"Sluice," said Slocum.

"That's him," the barkeep said. "Same man. When he got to town he called himself Callendar, but Mr. Grimes soon figured out he was really named Sluice."

"He had another man with him," Slocum said.

"Little bastard they call Jigs?"

"Yeah."

"We beat the shit out of him and sent him out of town."

The barkeep went on to detail the intended attack on the general store, how Sluice had run out on Jigs, and Jigs had later surrendered on Grimes's assurance that he would not be killed.

"Well," he continued, "we didn't kill him, but I bet he feels like he wished that we had."

"So Sluice went off first, and then Jigs," Slocum said.

"That's right."

"Well, I thank you for that information, pardner," Slocum said. Then he turned to Billy and said, "Let's sit down over yonder. I'm a little tuckered."

They moved to a nearby table with their bottle and glasses and sat down. Billy poured two more drinks.

"So," he said, "when we move out again, we're going to come across Jigs first."

"That's likely," Slocum said.

"Then we'll come upon Sluice."

"We'll most likely catch up with Grimes and them first," Slocum said. "We'll have to figure out how to deal with them."

"And what about Old Jan?"

"He's out there somewhere," Slocum said. "When we find him, maybe we'll have a better handle on how to proceed from there."

Old Jan reached the road and continued walking south. He was still leading the horse that Sluice had just about worn out. He still had his six-gun, but his rifle was in the boot on his horse, and Sluice had stolen his horse. He would have to be careful. He wondered how far back Slocum and Billy were. He wondered if they had yet left North Fork.

At long last, Jigs managed to get himself into the saddle. It hurt something awful, but he gritted his teeth and moaned and groaned out loud, and finally got it done. He managed to get the horse going and out onto the road, and he headed south. He had never before realized how much a horse bounced and rocked when it moved. Every motion hurt. He hoped that there was a town not too far ahead. He hoped that it would have a nice hotel, with a good place to eat and a good saloon. And a store with guns and ammunition. Yeah. He hoped that Sluice and Grimes had already gone through by the time he got there. He needed rest, and he needed protection.

Moving along, he came to a lane that turned to the left. It would not lead him to a town, but it might lead him to someplace where he could get some sympathy and some help. He turned down the lane. At the end of the lane, he found a small house. He noticed a fresh grave. But there was no sign of life. There was a corral, and he unsaddled his horse and put it in the corral. There was food and water in there for his horse. Everything he did caused him pain, but he knew that he would have to take care of his horse. It was all he had.

He staggered into the house and saw that it had been ransacked, but he rummaged through it again. He found some food, and he ate his fill. Then he found a loaded shotgun. He took the shotgun to the bed, propped it up there, and stretched himself out. It was not the softest bed he had ever experienced, but compared to the ground he had been using, it was luxurious. The little house was not a hotel room, but it would do nicely. Except for the pain that still tormented him, he was content—almost. He had food, for a little while. He had a gun. He would rather have had a rifle and a six-gun, but he had a gun. Most of all, he had a bed. He could lay up here for a while.

He did not have any whiskey, though, and he was very sorry for that. He had seen the empty bottle on the floor. Maybe there was some more somewhere. When he felt like it, he would get up and search more thoroughly. As he drifted off to sleep, he counted his blessings. He also counted the dangers he was still facing.

It wasn't long before Jigs heard the sound of approaching

horses. It brought him awake quick, and before he realized it, he had gotten himself up and onto his feet. It hurt like hell, but his sense of survival had taken over. He grabbed the shotgun and hurried to the door. It was Grimes and his whole goddamned outfit. He heard Grimes order two men to dismount and check out the cabin. He cocked the shotgun, jerked open the door, and fired both barrels. It jarred the hell out of him and knocked him back into the room, but the blast killed both men who had been walking toward the house. Grimes and the rest of the men scattered looking for cover. Jigs took advantage of the situation by running from the house and into the nearby thicket behind the corral. Crouching low, he realized that he had no more shotgun shells. He tossed the gun aside and moved deeper into the thicket.

12

Grimes and his men moved into the thicket looking for Jigs. This time Grimes's orders were to kill Jigs on sight. They moved slowly, guns ready. There were already two dead men in front of the small house, and, of course, they had no way of knowing that Jigs had no more shotgun shells on him. One man kicked something as he moved into the thicket. It did not feel like something that belonged in the thicket, so he stopped and looked down. He had kicked the shotgun that Jigs had discarded. He bent over and reached to pick it up. He did not see the snake, but he felt the hard hit and the bite. He straightened up, jerking his hand back.

"Ow. Goddamn," he said.

"What is it?" called another man who was not far away.

"Damn," the first man said. "I've been snakebit. Goddamn it to hell."

Soon, several men had gathered around him.

"Did you kill it?" said one.

"Hell, no. I never even seen it."

"It's still here somewhere," said another.

"Fucking snakes."

Grimes showed up about then. "Snakebit?" he said.

"My hand is already swelling up," said the snakebit man. "I'm going to die here."

"What kind of snake was it?" Grimes asked.

"Hell," said the wounded man, "I never seen it. But my hand is swelling up. Look at it."

"We'd better get him out of here," said Grimes.

"We'd better all of us get out of here," said another. "This fucking place could be infested with the goddamn things."

"Come on," said Grimes. He led the way back out to the clearing in front of the house. "Get him on his horse."

"I'm dizzy," the hurt man said.

"Someone get on behind him and hold him up," Grimes ordered.

"What about that goddamned Jigs in there?" said one man.

"Fuck him," said Grimes. "Let the snakes get him. Come on now. Let's get back to Bascomb in a hurry."

They rode out, leaving two dead men and two horses and Jigs still loose in the thicket. From his hiding place, Jigs had heard all this. He waited a short while, and then he came creeping out into the open. He saw the bodies of the two men he had killed with the shotgun. He saw their horses. Both horses had rifles in their saddle boots. Both dead men were wearing six-guns. One of them had two six-guns on him. Jigs counted his blessings once again. He was still hurting, in miserable pain, but he was well fed, and now he had a horse, two horses, and was well armed once again. And, of course, he still had his money.

He went back into the house and checked through it to see if there was anything he should take along with him. He found a little food and packed that in. He found a butcher knife and considered taking that along, but decided that it would be awkward to carry. He went back outside and pulled the gun belt off the man who'd been packing two guns. He strapped it around his waist. It was a little large for him, but at least it did not fall down around his knees. He went through the man's pockets and found some money, which he took. He found a box of bullets in the man's vest pocket, and he took them.

Then he went to the other body, and again he took the

gun, which he shoved into his waistband, and he also took
money and some more bullets. There would be other things
in the saddle rolls and saddlebags on the two horses. He took
the reins of one horse in his hands and mounted the other
horse, and he headed back for the road riding one good
horse and leading another. All he needed now was a good
room and a little time to lie around and recuperate. That and
a bottle of whiskey. But he did not know how far away the
next town was.

Old Jan plodded along. His feet were starting to hurt. He was
afraid he would have blisters all over them. He was not used to
walking any long distances. No cowboy was used to that. He
stopped and looked at the sorry horse he was leading. It looked
to him as if it would drop dead if he climbed on its back. It
needed more rest, more water, some good grass. Again, he
wondered how far back Billy and Slocum would be. And
he wondered how far ahead Sluice was. And Jigs was out
ahead of him too. Jigs would be moving more slowly, though.
Old Jan did not know, of course, what had happened with Jigs
back at the house. He did not know that Jigs was coming up
behind him riding a horse, moving more quickly now.

He plodded along, thinking that he and the horse he was
leading were about in the same sorry condition. Two old
wretches, both worn out, neither one long for the world, neither one worth much right now. It was interesting the way
things worked out in the world. Then he saw the stream that
sometimes ran along with the road, and sometimes disappeared off to the west somewhere. Now it was back near the
road. Old Jan decided on a rest—for him and for the horse.

"Come on, old fellow," he said, and he led the horse off
the road down to the stream and let it drink its fill. He, too,
had a drink of the fresh stream water. It was cold and it was
good. He looked back over his shoulder at the road, and he
did not like the fact that he was in full view of anyone passing by. He decided to move farther south along the stream
until it was well away from the road and covered by trees. If
Slocum and Billy came by, they would not see him, but then,

he figured he could still hear horses coming down the road. When he heard any, he would move through the trees and take a look. It should be all right, and he and the horse sure did need the rest.

The Grimes outfit was riding fast back north toward Bascomb when the man who was holding up the snakebit man called out. "Hey, Boss."

"What?" Grimes said over his shoulder.

"He's dead."

Grimes hauled back on his reins, slowing and then stopping his horse. The other riders stopped behind him. Grimes turned his horse to ride back to where the two men sat on the same horse. The one in the saddle was sagging.

"Dead?" Grimes said.

"Deader'n hell," said the other one.

"Well, shit," said Grimes. "Climb down off of there. Let's drag him to the side of the road."

They all dismounted, and two of the men dragged the body off the road and laid it out there as best they could. One of them looked over at Grimes. "What now, Boss?" he said.

"Hell," said Grimes, "we got no reason to go back to Bascomb now. We might just as well go on with what we were doing."

"Those two we're after are bad killers," said one of the men. "We left with ten of us. We're seven now."

"There's just two of them," said Grimes. "You suggesting that we can't handle two men?"

"No, sir. What I am suggesting, though, is that maybe we ought to move a little more slow and cautiouslike. You heard from that other man following them that they're ambushers along with everything else."

"Yeah," Grimes said. "You're right about that. We'll go slow. Right now, we'll find us a place to stop and eat a bite, drink some coffee, give our horses a rest. Then we'll move on."

Slocum and Billy were riding south along the main road when they saw a thin plume of smoke rising from off the west side of the road. Billy gestured toward it, and Slocum said, "I see it."

"What do we do?" Billy asked.

"Ride slow," said Slocum. "Try to spot them before they spot us."

"Who could it be?" asked Billy.

"I can't think," Slocum said. "Could be Jigs. He's moving slow from what we heard. It could be Old Jan waiting for us. On the other hand, it could be anyone. We won't know till we see them."

When they had gone a little farther down the road, Slocum stopped. He dismounted and took the Appaloosa's reins in his hand. "Let's walk from here," he said.

"Okay," said Billy, getting off his horse. They walked a little farther down the road until they saw seven men sitting around a small fire in the distance.

"Too many for Jigs or Old Jan," Slocum said. "Let's move a little closer."

"Hey," said Billy after a few more steps, "I recognize that Grimes."

"Yeah," said Slocum. "I see him."

"Do we say anything to them or just keep going?" Billy asked.

"Let's stop and have a visit," said Slocum, and they mounted their horses again and rode for the camp. When they came near to the camp, the seven men stood up. Three of them pulled out their revolvers.

"Hello there," Slocum called out. "Can we come in?"

"Ride up slow," answered Grimes.

The two riders approached the camp, and Grimes invited them to dismount. They did.

"My name's Slocum. This is my pardner, Billy Pierce," Slocum said.

"Grimes," said Grimes.

"We're trailing some men," said Slocum. "One of them's our pard. They call him Old Jan. He's keeping an eye out for a man named Sluice."

"I met your pard," said Grimes. "He's up there somewhere, I reckon. He left out of Bascomb before we did. That
Sluice, well, we're after that son of bitch ourselves."

"There was another man with him," said Slocum, "called
Jigs."

"Not anymore," Grimes said. "Seems like Sluice ran out
on Jigs back in Bascomb. When we got our hands on Jigs, we
beat the shit out of him. He's either crawled into a hole
somewhere to lick his wounds, or else he's after Sluice himself. We found Jigs in a house down the road a bit. He killed
two of my men. We'd have killed him, too, but one of my
men got bit by a snake and we were taking him back to town.
He croaked on us, so we turned around again to get after that
Sluice."

Slocum thought all that over. So Jigs, alone and beat up,
was somewhere ahead on the road. Old Jan was up there
somewhere, and presumably, Sluice was even farther along.
Now everything was complicated by Grimes and his bunch
on the same trail as Slocum and Billy and Old Jan. He considered asking Grimes how he and Sluice got crossways, but
he decided that was really none of his business.

"Sit down and have some coffee," Grimes said. Slocum
and Billy found seats around the fire, and one of Grimes's
men poured them each a cup of the hot, steaming coffee.
They sipped it in silence.

"I've heard about your manhunt from that ole man,"
Grimes said. "What did you call him?"

"Old Jan," said Billy.

"Yeah. Him. He stopped in Bascomb a time or two and
we talked. He told me how come you be chasing the bastard.
I reckon you got good reasons. Well, I got my good reasons,
too. Sluice and Jigs between the two of them have killed and
caused to be killed about seven of my men. Nicked my arm,
too. I mean to get them both, Slocum. So I'm suggesting to
you to stay out of my way."

"I don't want trouble with you, Grimes," Slocum said. "I
don't know you and I ain't got nothing against you. But if I

get to Sluice or Jigs ahead of you, I mean to kill them. Especially Sluice."

One of Grimes's men stood up and put his hand on his gun butt. "We could take them both out of our way right now, Boss," he said.

"Never mind that," said Grimes. "Sit down. These men are our guests right now."

The man sat down again, still looking gruff.

"Your boss just saved your life, mister," Slocum said.

"Hell," the man said, "there's seven of us here."

"I think I could get four before I dropped," said Slocum. "Billy could take out another two or three."

Grimes laughed. His six men looked at him like he was crazy. "He's likely right," he said. "Ain't none of you boys ever heard of Slocum?" No one responded. "Well, I have. I wouldn't go against Slocum with the six of you standing around me. From everything I've heard, he's fast and he's accurate, and he's survived a hell of a bunch of gunfights, several range wars, and I don't know what all else. He was right. I just saved your life. So just sit there and keep quiet and be thankful."

The man sat still and sulked, and Grimes continued talking. "Slocum, I'll try to get to them two before you do, but if you beat me to it, there won't be no trouble between you and me. Is that all right with you?"

"Sounds fair enough," Slocum said. He looked over at Billy. "What do you say, boy?"

"Sounds fair to me," Billy said.

Old Jan heard a horse coming down the road, and he hurried through the trees to get a look. After a short wait, he saw Jigs coming. Jigs was loaded down with guns, riding one good horse and leading another. The signs of the beating he had suffered were still visible. Old Jan did not have a rifle. He had only his six-gun. A shot would be too risky. He could see that the two horses were each carrying a rifle. Besides, Slocum might not like it if Old Jan took one of his targets away from him. Goddamn it, though, he would sure like to have one of those horses and one of those rifles.

Sluice came to the gate of a ranch house. He paused there in the road and considered the possibilities. A ranch would be well armed with a bunch of cowboys. If he rode in, he would have to be very careful of what he said, and he would have to be polite. But they would have food and coffee and maybe even whiskey. They would also be able to tell him how far it was to the next town. He decided that he could be careful and polite if he had to. He turned his horse onto the lane that led west to the big ranch house. He was about halfway to the house when two riders came up to him.

"Howdy," he said.

"What you want here, stranger?" said one of the riders.

"A little hospitality," said Sluice. "That's all."

The two cowboys looked at each other. Sluice noticed that both were rugged-looking men, and both wore their guns low on their hips. If they told him to turn around and hightail it out of there, he damn sure would do it.

"Look," he said, "if it ain't convenient, I'll just turn around and ride on out."

One of the men leaned over and spoke low to his partner. Then they both straightened up again.

"Come on," one of the two said. "Cookie'll just about have a meal ready."

"Thanks," said Sluice. The cowboys turned their horses and led the rest of the way to the main house, then past the house to a cookshack just beyond. There was a corral nearby.

"Turn your horses loose in there," one said. "Come with us."

With the horses unsaddled and turned into the corral, Sluice followed the two hands into the cookshack, where there was a long table with men sitting all around it. The two hands motioned to a chair, and Sluice sat down, thanking them. The men around the long table all gave Sluice hard stares. He was more than a bit uneasy. Then the door opened again, and a man wearing good rancher's clothing stepped inside. He spotted Sluice right away, and a smile spread over his face.

"Sluice," he said. "You old son of a bitch. How the hell are you?"

13

Sluice stood up, a wide grin spreading across his face. He held his arms out wide as the other man approached him. They shared a hearty bear hug, laughing and slapping each other on the back.

"Reb," said Sluice. "Reb Gillian. Goddamn. I ain't seen you for a goddamned coon's age. Or two. What the hell are you doing in these parts?"

"Hell. This is my spread, you old fart," said Gillian. "My headquarters."

"You own this place?" asked Sluice.

"Lock, stock, and barrel. There ain't even a note on it. It's all mine."

"Well, how the hell—"

"Never mind that right now," Gillian said. "Food's ready. Sit back down. I'll sit by you. Pete, move down yonder, will you?"

"Sure, Boss," said the man called Pete. He got up and moved to another unoccupied chair, and Sluice and Gillian sat down. The cook came out and started dishing out the meal. Gillian was the first one served. Sluice was next. They both started shoveling it in as soon as they got it. Everyone else was served, though, pretty quickly.

"You was about to ask me just how the hell I was to come by a place like this, wasn't you?" Gillian asked Sluice.

"Yeah," said Sluice. "Something like that."

"Well, it was easy. You know, you can run on for years struggling to get your hands on something, and when you finally get hold of it, it was just like someone dumped it in your lap."

"That easy?"

"Damn near. You hear about that range war up north just a while back?"

"Up in Wyoming? Yeah. I heard the big ranchers lost out. Is that right?"

"The big boys had me and ole Slocum working for them. We was trying to get rid of squatters, so we told Slocum they was a bunch of rustlers. Well, he was with us for a spell, but then he figured out the truth of it, and he went and switched sides. Things turned on us real fast. He's that good. Well, my boss, he called me in one day, and he said that he had a place down south—this place here he was talking about—and he said that if I would promise to stick with him till the bitter end, he would sign it over to me. And he did, too. I stuck with him, too. He got hisself killed eventual. It was then I took off and come down here to see what I had. I got all these boys together, and we got us a hell of a layout." He leaned over close to Sluice as if he was about to impart a big secret, even though everyone in the room already knew about it. "We run off a bunch of cattle or a bunch of horses, we got a perfect place to keep them till we can sell them. We ride off someplace to pull some kind of a job, say a bank or a stagecoach, we got a perfect hideout and a good excuse for having money. I'm a big rancher. Everyone expects me to have dough, and they expect my hands to have dough. It's a sweet setup."

"By damn," said Sluice. "I'd say so."

"What have you got going, ole pard?"

"Aw," Sluice said, "I ain't got nothing just now. I've still got some bucks in my pocket from the last job I pulled, but right now I'm sort of in between. You know what I mean?"

"I know. Well, hell, pardner, why don't you come in with me? I've knowed you longer than any of these boys here. We've rode some hard trails together, ain't we?"

"Yeah," Sluice said, "we sure as hell have. I'll never forget them, not as long as I live."

"Me neither," said Gillian. "Well, hell, what do you say?"

"I say hell, yes. Hell, yes, old pard. It was a real stroke of luck coming on you like this."

Jigs was riding slowly, still leading the extra horse. He was feeling weak again, and his old injuries were hurting him. He was also hungry and wishing that a town would magically appear on the horizon. Instead, he came across a lane turning west with a large arched gateway. He could see a ranch house in the distance. A ranch. They would feed him. Ranchers were like that. They were generous and hospitable. They were— Hell, damn, he thought. Sluice could be in there. He did not feel like running into Sluice just then. He wondered what to do. If he passed by the ranch, he might get ahead of Sluice, and he did not want that. But the other angle was that he would almost for sure pass up a good meal, and he had no idea how much farther he would have to ride to find another one.

He wanted Sluice, but he wanted to come up behind him with a good rifle shot. He had no intention of giving Sluice a fair and even chance. The son of a bitch did not deserve such consideration, not after what he had done to Jigs— twice. He deserved to be shit on. He deserved to be skinned alive. Jigs imagined Sluice hanging upside down and naked on a barn door, and Jigs there in front of him with a skinning knife and a pair of pliers. He could imagine no greater pleasure.

At last, partly because he felt he could go no farther, he decided to move across the road from the ranch gate and make a small camp. No fire. There was thicket enough to hide in, and he could watch the gate. He could wait and see if Sluice would come riding out. He had two rifles. He also still had some of the food he had taken from the small house back down the road. It wasn't the best fare, but he would not starve. He moved into the thicket.

Farther back down the road, Old Jan was plodding along, still leading the sorry horse Sluice had abandoned. His feet were tormenting him and his leg muscles were sore. He spotted a proper-sized boulder by the side of the road, and decided to sit on it. He needed a bit of a rest. He took off his hat and wiped his forehead with his right sleeve. He had been sitting there a few minutes and was about to decide to start walking again, when he heard the sound of approaching horses. He stood up, pulled out his six-gun, and led the wretched horse off the road a short ways. He waited. When the riders showed up, he recognized Slocum and Billy Pierce. He stepped out into view.

"It's Old Jan," said Billy.

"Howdy Billy, Slocum," Old Jan said. "It's sure good to see you boys."

"What happened to your horse?" Slocum asked.

Old Jan told the tale of what had happened in Bascomb, of setting out after Sluice and Jigs, and of his chance encounter with Sluice on the lane to the small house. He told them that Sluice and Jigs were separated, but they were still both ahead of them on the road.

"Lucky you came out of that okay," said Billy Pierce.

"Okay except for my horse," Old Jan said. "The bastard rode off with mine and left this worn-out nag behind. I've been walking ever since then."

"He looks like you could ride him now," said Slocum, "as long as you don't drive him too hard."

"Yeah," said Old Jan. "You should have seen the poor wretch when I first picked him up. He was nearly dead."

"Grimes and about six of his cowboys are pretty close behind us," Slocum said. "We need to move out pretty damn soon."

"Well," said Old Jan, "I'm ready. I don't know if I can say the same for this old horse."

They all mounted and started riding. As long as they

moved slowly, the old horse did all right. Old Jan had made sure that it got its rest and got enough to eat and drink.

"So what's going to happen if Grimes and them catches up with us?" asked Old Jan.

"He told us there wouldn't be no trouble between us," Billy Pierce said.

"I don't think he'll try to ride through us," Slocum said.

"He's afraid of Slocum," Billy said, a wide grin on his face.

"Speaking of that sort of thing," said Old Jan, "how are you, Slocum? How's your gun arm? Your endurance?"

"I'm all right," Slocum said. "I'll handle myself just fine."

Gillian called Sluice into the private office in his big ranch house. He gave him a cigar and a glass of whiskey. They sat down in easy chairs.

"Damn good cigar, Reb," said Sluice. "Good whiskey, too."

"Nothing but the best," said Gillian. "But now, listen. You're going to be the first to know. I've got a big job planned. We'll be riding out in the morning. All but four of us. I'll leave four behind to keep an eye on things here."

"That makes good sense," Sluice said. "But what's the job?"

"I got word about a gold shipment leaving a bank over in Colorado. I know the route they'll be taking. I know how many guards will be along with it. We have the men to take it. Believe me."

"Sounds good to me," Sluice said. "I'm with you."

"Hell, I knew you would be," said Gillian. "I'll give you all the details when I talk to the rest of the boys. For right now, though, we'll take off early. Before first light."

"I'll be ready," said Sluice.

It was early the next morning when Jigs was awakened by the sounds of a bunch of riders. He sat up and sneaked to the edge of the road, where he saw Sluice riding with nine other men. They came down the lane to the road and turned south. They were heavily armed and looked ready for action. Jigs wondered where they were going and how long they would be gone. He watched until they disappeared along the road. Then it occurred to him that there would be no more than a few men left on the ranch, and none of them would know him at all. He could go over there and get a good hot meal and coffee, plenty of hot coffee. He could have himself well fed and get out again before Sluice and the others returned. He hurried back to saddle his horse.

Jigs mounted up and rode across the road and through the gateway. Soon, he had reached the big ranch house. Just as he was about to dismount, two cowboys showed up and approached him. "Howdy there," he said. "Can I get down?"

"Sure, climb on down," said one.

"What are you doing here?" said the other one.

"I was just passing by," Jigs said. "I thought that maybe I could get a meal and some coffee here."

"Sure. Why not," said one of the cowboys. "Tie up your horse and come along with me."

Jigs tied the horse and followed the two cowhands to the cookshack. They indicated a chair for him, and he sat down. Pretty soon he had eggs and ham, biscuits, gravy, and coffee in front of him. He ate like a man who had been starved, and he drank four cups of coffee. He put several spoonfuls of sugar in each cup. One of the cowhands sat down across the table from Jigs, and when he saw that Jigs had finished eating, he spoke.

"Say, pal," he said. "I hope you don't mind me asking, but what the hell happened to you? You look a damn mess."

"Yeah, I reckon I do at that," Jigs said. "I don't mind you asking. I was in a little town back down the road. Name of Bascomb. Got into it with the locals. One of them shot my damn nose off. It hurt like hell, I can tell you. Still hurts some. Then they had me surrounded and outnumbered. I agreed to come out and surrender if they'd let me ride out. They said okay, but when I come out they beat the shit out of me. A whole bunch of them."

"That's a rotten deal," said the cowboy.

"I think they're on the road after me," Jigs said.

"You mean, with what all they done to you, they still ain't satisfied?"

"I reckon not," Jigs said.

"How many of them are they?"

"Five or six, I think," Jigs said. "I better not hang around here too long. They might show up just any time."

"Hey. Our boss and most of the boys are off on a job. They left four of us here to watch the ranch. It's kind of boring around here. Four of us and one of you makes five. Right? Why don't you stay here with us? If those chicken-shits show up, we'll help you take them out. What do you say?"

"You'd do that for me?" said Jigs. "How come?"

"Like I said, it gets boring around here. And I don't like the story of how they done you."

"Slocum," said Old Jan. "There's riders coming up behind us."

"Let's move off the road and let them pass," Slocum said.

"What if it's Grimes?" said Billy. "You said—"

"I changed my mind," said Slocum. "I don't want them so close behind us."

They rode their horses off the road and out of sight and waited. Sure enough, it was Grimes and his crew. Slocum and his friends watched while the small gang rode past them. Then they moved back out onto the road.

Something about the four cowhands made Jigs think that he could trust them. He decided to take a chance and tell them more.

"You know," he said, "I didn't tell you even half of my story."

"You mean there's more?" said a puncher they called Limpy.

"Yeah," said Jigs. "Back in that Bascomb, I had me a pard. Well, to tell you the truth, he had run out on me once before. I caught up with him meaning to kill him, but he talked his way out of it. He had this scheme to take over the town, and he said I was in on it. Well, he jumped the gun. He killed a man before he should have and got the rest of them down on us. They come after us. We was holed up in a general store. He was in the back room when they come at us, and he run out on me again. That's when they beat me up like this. Like I told you."

"Damn," said Limpy. "That's a rotten chickenshit thing to do to a pard."

"I been chasing him to get even, but I ain't caught him yet."

"This man have a name?" asked one of the other cowboys.

"He's called Sluice," said Jigs.

The four cowboys fell silent and looked at one another.

"Something wrong?" said Jigs.

"Sluice is our boss's good buddy," said Limpy. "He rode out with the rest of them this morning to do that job."

"Oh, hell," said Jigs. "I'm sorry. I didn't know. I guess I'll be moving along then. I won't hold you to what you said about helping me."

"No," said Limpy, "hell, hold on. We'll still do what we said we'd do. It's just that, we'll have to think about what to do after that. What to do about Sluice."

Jigs paused a bit before making his next statement. He had stuck his neck out thus far, though, so he went ahead. "You know," he said, "with Sluice involved, I'd say that job you been talking about is something just a bit shady."

"They're holding up a gold shipment," said Limpy.

"Hey, Limpy," said another of the cowhands, "you ought to watch your goddamned mouth."

"Aw, hell," said Limpy, "Jigs here has rode with Sluice. He knows what's what. Ain't no harm done."

"He's right, boys," Jigs said. "I ain't going to say nothing. Hell, you boys has been awful good to me."

"You know, Limpy," said another cowboy, one who had been quiet all this time, "now that we know more about that fucking Sluice, I ain't so sure I like Reb bringing him in like he done. A man who'd run out on his pardner like that ain't worth a shit."

"So what are we going to do when they get back?" asked yet another of the men. "We going to call the boss on it?"

"I don't know," Limpy said. "We might. I feel like we ought to. I just don't know yet."

14

Sluice, Gillian, and the rest of Gillian's gang lay in wait along both sides of a small road in Colorado, waiting for the stage that would be carrying the gold Gillian had advance knowledge about. Gillian and Sluice were side by side behind a small boulder. Gillian was smoking a handmade cigarette.

"Reb," said Sluice, "are you sure you got the right information about that shipment?"

"Couldn't be more sure," said Gillian. "It's good information all right."

"I can't tell you how good it is to be working with you again, Reb," Sluice said. "I've been stuck with fucking idiots ever since we split up."

Gillian laughed. "About the same here, ole pard," he said. He lowered his voice. "Like this bunch I've got now. They ain't worth much. The only good thing about it is that as long as I pay them, they do what I say."

"I know what you mean," Sluice agreed.

"Well, hell, Sluice," Gillian said, "come to think of it, anyone who'd work for me or for you can't be worth much of a shit, can he?" They both laughed at that. "What's good about you and me is that we don't one of us work for the other one. We work together."

"You said it all right," Sluice concurred. "Hey. Wait a minute. I think I hear something coming."

They sat quiet for a moment until the unmistakable sounds of a coach and horses could be heard. All of the men pulled out their six-guns and waited. Finally, the coach came into sight. There was a driver and a shotgun rider on top. Sluice and Gillian could not tell about passengers, but two more armed men rode alongside the coach. Guards. Of course. Sluice thought that Gillian had to be right about this. Why else would a coach be traveling with armed guards?

"Sluice," said Gillian.

"Yeah?"

"Ease down to your left and tell Harvey to use his rifle. Tell him to pick off the driver and the shotgun."

"Gotcha," Sluice answered.

He scooted off to his left until he came to where Harvey was hidden. "Reb says pick off the driver and the shotgun," he told him. "Use your rifle."

Harvey holstered his six-gun and picked up his rifle. He cranked a shell into the chamber and took careful aim. He waited a moment till the coach came closer, and then he squeezed the trigger. The driver gave a jerk and slumped in the seat. Harvey cranked another shell and took quick aim, firing a second shot, which knocked the shotgun rider off the coach. The man was dead by the time he hit the road. The body bounced a few times and then lay still. The coach, now driverless, raced wildly on down the road.

"Take some boys and go get it," Gillian said to Sluice.

Sluice hurried to gather some help and chase the runaway coach. By the time they were all mounted and riding, the coach was out of sight. They rode hard after it. The two mounted guards had dismounted and taken cover at the first shot. Gillian and the remaining outlaws stayed hidden and fired wild shots at the two men. Now and then, the two guards returned fire. Mostly, the men on either side did not have good shots at their opponents. All parties were well dug in.

Farther on down the road, Sluice and two outlaw riders

caught up with the wildly careening coach. The two riders caught the lead horses by their harness. Sluice climbed up onto the seat and gathered the reins. "Whoa. Whoa," he called out. Soon, the horses were settled down. Sluice looked under the seat and found nothing. One of the outlaw riders opened the door to the coach, and found himself facing another special guard who had been hidden in the coach. The guard fired, striking the outlaw in the neck. The flabbergasted outlaw, head bouncing ludicrously, slowly sagged from his saddle and fell onto the hard-packed road. Sluice dropped off the coach on the other side and fired a bullet into the guard's back.

The remaining outlaw turned his horse and hurried to where his partner had fallen. The man was still lying there, kicking and gurgling.

"Bart?" said the outlaw.

"He's dead," said Sluice, "or will be soon."

"He's still alive," said the outlaw.

Sluice moved through the coach to the doorway nearest the wounded man. He thumbed back the hammer on his revolver, aimed, and fired a shot into the man's heart. The twitching and the gurgling stopped. The man was dead. The remaining outlaw looked at Sluice in disbelief.

"I just put him out of his misery is all," said Sluice. "I'd do the same for you. Now let's find that fucking gold."

Back at the gunfight, Reb Gillian was getting frustrated. He snaked his way down to Harvey.

"We ain't getting nowhere here," he said. "We can't see them, and they can't see us."

"We're just wasting bullets," said Harvey. "You got any ideas?"

"We got to draw their fire, so we can see where they're at," said Gillian. "I want you to run across the road."

"Me?"

"It'll be all right," Gillian said. "If you move fast, they won't have time to aim. Duck low and run like hell. Head for that big tree over there. As soon they show their damn heads, we'll start shooting. You got it?"

"Yeah," Harvey said. "I got it all right."

Harvey took several deep breaths, then stood up suddenly in a crouching position and ran for all he was worth, zigzagging across the road. As soon as he moved, one of the guards popped up from behind a rock. Gillian and a couple other outlaws fired, and the guard dropped out of sight. The sound of the shots was like a spur in Harvey's butt. His speed increased considerably, but just before he was about to duck behind the big tree, the other guard showed himself and fired a rifle shot that hit Harvey in the back, causing him to tumble forward and wind up on his shoulders with his legs sticking up the side of the tree trunk. He did not move. He was dead.

At the same time, Gillian and the others fired at the second guard. The guard, like the first one, disappeared. Finally, the shooting stopped. After a few quiet moments, Gillian called out, "Boys. Get down there and make sure them two are dead." There was a little hesitation, but the men began showing themselves. Slowly, guns ready, they walked down the road, mostly along one of the sides. Gillian waited till they had all walked past his position before he exposed himself. Then he stood up and walked behind them. The first of the gang to reach the area where the guards had been hidden finally called out, "This one's done for." In another minute, a shot was fired. "So is this one," another man yelled.

"Mount up," said Gillian. "Let's go find that coach."

Sluice had just jerked open the rear boot on the stage when Gillian and the rest came riding up. He had exposed a large locked box. Gillian pulled up beside him and dismounted. The others dismounted and crowded around Sluice and Gillian. Gillian pulled out his six-shooter and said, "Stand back."

They all backed off as Gillian fired, busting the lock. Sluice moved in quickly, throwing the top back to reveal bags. Gillian grabbed one of the bags and fumbled with the tie, at last getting it open. He shoved a hand in and came out with a fistful of gold coins, which he displayed to all. A general cheer rose up from the gang. Gillian dumped the coins back into the bag and tied the string again. He pulled out two of the heavy bags and held them toward one of the outlaws.

"Put these on your horse," he said. The man took them and staggered away under the weight. Then Gillian handed out two more bags, and two more, until all of the bags of gold were tied onto horses. He was out of gold bags before he got to his own horse or to Sluice's horse. Sluice gave him a questioning look, and Gillian smiled and said in a low voice, "Don't worry. They'll all get to the ranch safely."

Grimes and his small gang arrived at the Gillian ranch, not knowing, of course, whose it was. Grimes stopped in the middle of the road and stared for a moment at the gateway. Finally, he spoke.

"Let's check in here and find out if anyone's stopped by," he said.

"Sure, Boss," one of the men answered.

They turned and headed down the lane toward the ranch headquarters. Down the lane inside the house, Limpy looked out and saw them coming.

"Hey, Jigs," he said. "Come here."

"What?" said Jigs, hurrying over to join Limpy at the window.

"Do you know them that's coming?" Limpy asked.

Jigs pressed his face against the windowpane.

"Goddamn," he said. "That there's Grimes. Him I told you about. He's the one that had me beat up. I knowed he'd be after me."

"Well," said Limpy, "there's seven of them, and there's five of us. It seems to me like we've got the edge. We're in the house and they're out in the open. We know who they are, and they don't know that you're in here. They don't know us. We sure as hell won't let them get you, friend."

The riders came closer, and Limpy stepped out on the porch.

"Hold on there," he yelled.

"Hold it, boys," said Grimes, halting his own mount. The

other six pulled up behind him. "Just seven travelers passing by," he said to Limpy. "Looking for ranch hospitality."

"Well," said Limpy, "ordinarily you'd get some, but the boss, he went off for a few days and left us shorthanded. His orders was to let nobody stop over."

"Well," said Grimes, "could we maybe at least water our horses?"

"Trough's over there by the corral," Limpy said. "Go on ahead, and get it over with."

Grimes urged his horse toward the corral and his men followed him. "Come along, boys," he said. Then louder, he said, "Thank you, friend."

The seven men rode to the trough. Two of them let their horses drink. "Don't hurry it up now," said Grimes. "Take your time."

The horses drank their fill, and the next two were moved up to drink. There were still three horses left. Meanwhile, one of Grimes's men was staring at the house, but he was not looking at Limpy standing on the porch. He saw Jigs's face pressed against the glass of a windowpane.

"Boss," he said.

"What?" Grimes answered.

"Jigs is in there."

"In the house?"

"Yeah. He's looking out the window to the right of the front door."

Grimes took hold of his saddle horn, put his foot in the stirrup, and swung himself into the saddle. When he did so, he allowed his horse to turn in a circle, and while the animal was turning, he looked toward the house. He saw Jigs there in the window.

"He's right, boys," he said. "They're hiding Jigs. That's why they wouldn't let us stop over."

The last horse was watered, and the other six men mounted up.

"What're we going to do, Boss?" asked one of the men.

"See them bales of hay out in front of the house?" Grimes said. "Head for them."

They started riding back toward the road, but as they were about to pass the house, Grimes yelled and kicked his horse in the sides, heading for the hay bales. The others followed him. Behind the bales, they dismounted quickly and ran for the cover of the hay bales, allowing their horses to run loose. When they did that, Limpy turned and ran back into the house, slamming the door behind him. He went to a window and opened it so he could yell out.

"What the hell are you up to?" he shouted.

"You're hiding Jigs in there," Grimes yelled. "Send him out, and we'll ride away."

"We ain't sending nobody out," Limpy shouted.

"I'll give you a little time to think about that," said Grimes, "before we start shooting."

"Shoot away, you son of a bitch," Limpy said, and he fired the first shot. His bullet buried itself harmlessly in the hay. Grimes and his six men started returning fire instantly, peppering the front of the ranch house and shattering every pane of glass in the windows. All the cowhands inside ducked down close to the floor. No one was hit.

"Hold your fire, boys," said Grimes. The shooting stopped. After the loud barrage of shots, the silence was ominous. Grimes and his men were huddled up low behind the stack of hay bales, safely out of sight of the men in the house. But if they stayed that way, they would be in a stalemate that could last forever. The men inside had food, shade, chairs, and beds.

"What're we going to do, Boss?" asked one of Grimes's men.

"I don't quite know, Red," said Grimes. "Give me a few minutes to think on it."

"Boss?" said Red.

"What is it?"

"I got me a idea."

"All right," said Grimes. "Tell me about it."

"See that old wagon over yonder?"

"Sure. I see it."

"I think I could work my way over there real slowlike by dragging one of these bales along."

"Yeah?"

Once I get there and have the wagon as cover, I could shove the bale up into the wagon. I got some matches in my pocket. I could—"

"Light the hay on fire and shove the wagon up against the house," said Grimes with a grin on his face. "Is that where you were going?"

"That's just where I was going," said Red.

"All right then," said Grimes. "Go to it."

Red grabbed hold of one of the top bales of hay and started pulling on it. Two other men gave him a hand. Soon the bale toppled over onto the ground. Staying behind the bale, Red began to move it. It moved only a few inches at a time, but it moved.

Inside the house, Jigs was looking out a window. "What the hell are they up to?" he said. Limpy came running to his side.

"Where?" he said.

"Look," said Jigs. "That there hay bale weren't out there away from the stack like that. Were it?"

"By God," said Limpy, "you're right. They're moving it."

"Well, how come?"

"Maybe they're just trying to get up closer," Limpy said.

"Only thing is, they ain't getting closer. They're just kind of sidling along there."

"Well, they got to be up to something," Limpy said. "Let's see if we can stop them. Boys, empty your guns into that lone hay bale out there."

The five men in the house unleashed a salvo of bullets into the bale of hay, and when they did, Red scrunched up as near to the ground as he could get. He would have laid himself flat on the ground, but he was afraid if he did that, part of his body would show somewhere. As soon as Grimes figured out what was happening, he issued a new order.

"Shoot those windows," he called out.

Grimes and his men behind the stack of bales started firing at the windows. One of the men inside yelped and dropped to the floor. "I'm hit," he cried out. "I'm hit."

The rest of the men ducked low again. The firing stopped. The lone hay bale inched along again.

15

Red at last made his way to the wagon. He lay low for a moment, taking deep breaths. Then he stood up, grabbed hold of the bale, and heaved it up into the wagon bed. Some shots were fired at him, but another barrage from Grimes and the other men stopped it. Red pulled a match out of his pocket and struck it on the side of the wagon. He cupped his hands around it and held it to the hay bale. When he had a fire going, he hurried to the front end of the wagon and taking hold of the tongue, maneuvered the wagon toward the side of the house. When he had it aimed properly, he began to push. It went easily. It rolled smoothly and picked up speed. Red was soon running behind the wagon. And then it smashed against the side of the house. Red stayed there waiting. He watched until the flames had caught the wall and began inching their way up the side. Then he ran to the front corner of the house and gestured to Grimes that he was going to run around to the back. Then he ran.

Behind the hay bales, Grimes watched gleefully as the flames crept up the wall. Then he said, "All right, boys. Before long, those bastards will start running out of the house. Red's watching the back door. We'll watch the front. When they come out, shoot them."

Inside the house, smoke began creeping in through the

cracks in the wall and around the windows. "They're burning us out," said Limpy.

"The dirty bastards," said Jigs. "They'd burn us alive."

"In just a few minutes," said Limpy, "we'll have to leave the house."

"We can go out the back way," said another of the men.

"They'll have that covered," said Limpy. "Likely, the son of a bitch that set the fire."

"Well, he's only one man. There's several out front."

"Yeah," Limpy agreed. "Let's not wait. Let's make a run for it. Now. Fire a couple of shots out the front window first."

The other man fired two shots at the hay bales, then ran for the back door. The men out front fired another barrage at the windows. Inside, the first two men ran out the back door. From the corner of the house, Red fired a shot, dropping the first man. The second fired a snap shot at Red, who ducked back around the corner. A third man, the one who had been hit before, ran out and kept running. Red peeked around the corner again, but the second man out was still there, and he fired again. Red ducked back again. Flames were licking high on the wall of the house by this time, and Red suddenly realized that he would not be able to hide there for much longer. Jigs came out then and ran like hell, and finally Limpy stepped out.

"Let's go," he said, and he and the man who had been firing to cover them ran after the other two. They all ended up in the middle of an open field, vast and flat. It was grassland, good for grazing cattle, but not worth a damn for hiding. They stood there watching flames engulf the house.

"What'll we do now, Limpy?" asked the wounded man.

"Here," said Limpy. "Let me tie a rag around that wound."

"Ouch," said the man as Limpy wrapped his bandanna around the nicked upper left arm and pulled it tight. "What're we going to do?"

"Those farts are still out there," Limpy said. "We got no rifles, no horses."

"They'll come looking for us pretty soon," the man said.

"Lay down flat," Limpy said. "They won't see us in the tall grass."

Meanwhile, Red ran back around to the front of the burning house. "Grimes," he called out. "They got out the back way. I got one of them, but the rest are out there in back."

"Come on, boys," said Grimes. "Mount up."

Grimes's men, including Red, all hurried to their horses and climbed into their saddles, pulling the rifles out of the boots and cranking shells into the chambers. Grimes led the way around the blazing house. Behind it, they stopped. They looked around. They saw nothing. Grimes looked at Red.

"Where the hell are they?" he said.

Red swept his arm at the grassy field beyond. "Out there somewhere," he said.

"Let's ride out there and get them," said one of the men.

"No," said Grimes. "They got no rifles or else they'd be trying to pick us off right now. We're out of their pistol range. If we go riding out there looking for them, we lose that advantage."

"So what do we do?"

"Take the horses off to the side there," Grimes said. "We'll just stay here and watch. We can last longer than they can."

Out in the field, Jigs started inching his way through the tall grass, moving in the direction of the corral and the cook-shack. He was grateful for the slight breeze that was causing the grass to wave. Perhaps his movements would not be detected. Even so, it was going to take him a hell of a long time to get there. He had two six-guns on him and a belt, its loops almost all stuffed with shells. As he crawled along, all of his bumps and bruises and scrapes and cracked ribs started hurting him again. He crept on.

The flames were roaring by this time. Grimes and his six men moved farther away from the intense heat. They stopped off to their right, not venturing any farther out into the grass-land behind the house. They kept watching the grass for any signs, but nothing betrayed the whereabouts of Jigs and his new friends. One man dug into his pack for a biscuit and a piece of jerky. Another rolled himself a cigarette and lit it. Yet another busied himself wiping down his rifle with a rag. Grimes paced, keeping his eyes on the field of grass.

The roof of the house suddenly caved in, sending flames and sparks shooting up high into the sky for a brief instant. The flames died down again but continued burning low. Smoke was billowing up high into the sky before dissipating into the clouds. The crackling was loud, and now and then there came a loud popping sound. The wind shifted slightly, but enough to cause the smoke to drift toward Grimes and his bunch.

"I like the smell of burning wood," one man said.

"You mean the smell of a burning house," said another.

The men all laughed at that. Grimes had stopped pacing. He was sitting on the ground on the shady side of one of the horses. Red moved over and sat beside him. He pulled a plug out of his pocket and took a chaw.

"Boss," he said. Grimes turned his head and looked at him. "Boss, we don't have to just set here and wait."

"What you got in mind?" asked Grimes.

"We got plenty of ammo," said Red. "We could just set right here and sort of sweep that field with rifle shots. We might hit someone, but even if we didn't, we'd for pretty damn certain spook them out."

Grimes smiled a half smile. "That's a pretty good idea, Red. Go ahead and line up the boys and get it going."

"Limpy," said the wounded man out in the grass. "Limpy."

"What is it?" Limpy answered.

"Limpy, we have a clear view of them bastards from here."

"They're out of six-gun range," Limpy answered. "Ain't nothing we can do right now except stay down. We can see them, but they can't see us."

"Well, look at them. They're lining up right now with rifles."

Limpy could see them, and he also was getting nervous, wondering just what the hell they were up to. He was sure that they couldn't see where the men in the grass were hidden. Just then, the riflemen opened up. Limpy covered his head with his hands. The shots all hit the ground several feet in front of him.

"Goddamn," he said.

Off to their right, Jigs was still crawling through the grass. He heard the shots, and he twisted his head to get a look. He could see Grimes's men with their rifles. He could see that they were shooting into the grass. He was damn glad that he had started sneaking away when he did. He decided that with all the shooting going on, he could move a little faster. Everyone's attention was on the shooting, either on the shooters or on the part of the field they were shooting into. He quickened his pace, still careful to keep his ass low to the ground.

Out on the road, Slocum, Old Jan, and Billy Pierce were still riding along headed south when they heard the shots coming from somewhere up ahead. They glanced at one another, then spurred their horses.

"What the hell could that be?" Billy yelled.

"Let's find out," answered Slocum.

They rode hard until the shots sounded close, and then they slowed their mounts and moved ahead cautiously. Then they came to the gateway leading to the ranch house. Slocum halted his Appaloosa and held up a hand for the other two to stop as well. He looked toward the still-rising black smoke.

"It's coming from over there," he said.

"Looks like someone's torched a house, too," said Old Jan.

"Come on," said Slocum. "But go slow and keep your eyes open."

They turned onto the lane and headed for the smoldering ruins of the ranch house. More shots sounded. They were close now. Slocum pointed toward the smoke.

"They're coming from over there," he said.

They reached the hay bales that were in front of what used to be the house.

"Leave the horses here," Slocum said.

They dismounted and pulled their rifles out of the boots. Then they started moving toward the shots, careful to keep themselves hidden behind the smoldering ruins. Rounding the front corner of the heap, Slocum spotted the riflemen. He motioned Billy and Old Jan to follow him and moved carefully toward the men. One man was not shooting. He was just watching, like a field officer in the army. He turned his head slightly and Slocum recognized him.

"Grimes," he shouted.

Grimes turned to see who had called his name.

"Slocum?"

Slocum aimed his Winchester at Grimes. "Tell your men to stop that shooting," he said.

"Hold your fire, men," said Grimes.

Slocum and his two pards walked over to Grimes. Slocum was no longer aiming at Grimes, but he held his rifle ready.

"Slocum, I thought you were ahead of me," Grimes said.

"Yeah, well, that's what I wanted you to think. What the hell's going on here?"

"We came on Jigs," Grimes said. "Some cowpokes here were hiding him. They were in the house, but we chased them out there in the grass."

"You burned them out?" said Slocum.

"That's right," said Grimes. "We burned them out. Red got one of them as they came out the back door, but Jigs and the rest got away. Sort of. We have them pinned down out there."

"You got anything against these cowboys?" Slocum asked.

"I just want Jigs," said Grimes.

"Don't do any more shooting for a spell," Slocum said, and he walked out in front of the riflemen a few paces.

"Keep holding your fire, boys," Grimes said.

"Hey, you, out there in the grass," Slocum called out. "My name's Slocum. I just got here. I ain't one of them that's been shooting at you. Can you hear me?"

There was a long moment of silence before Limpy decided to answer.

"What do you want, Slocum?"

"I want the same thing these other men want," Slocum said. "I want Jigs. That's all I want. I ain't got nothing against you. Send Jigs out here, and I'll call off these shooters."

From where he was nearing the corral, Jigs could hear the talking from both sides. He wondered if he could survive if he was to tell them what Sluice was up to. It was worth a thought, but he was too afraid to try it. He kept moving.

"I promised him protection," Limpy called back.

"He was part of a gang that murdered my boss and one of my pardners," Slocum said. "Shot me and left me for dead. I mean to get him. I don't want to hurt no one else if I don't have to."

"Hey, Limpy," said one of the other hands out in the field. "He's got a good reason. Give him Jigs. It won't hurt us none."

"He said he'd let us go," said the other one.

"Slocum," yelled Limpy.

"I'm here."

"Slocum, can you give me and the boys a couple of minutes to talk it over?"

"Take five," said Slocum.

Jigs reached the edge of the high grass. He was very close to the cookshack. He stayed on his belly and inched his way to the shack, feeling very relieved to stand up on his feet once again. He sucked in a few deep breaths and walked the length of the shack. The bastards would not have a good view of him from here on, but he would have to be quiet. He walked to the corral and went inside. He saddled a horse and led it out of the corral. Then, mounting up, he started riding slowly, guiding the horse in an easterly direction across the prairie.

"Slocum," Limpy yelled. "If I stand up to talk to you, will they hold their fire?"

Slocum looked back at Grimes. "They will," he said. Grimes nodded in agreement. Out in the field, Limpy stood up. He was holding his hands out to his sides. Slocum walked toward him. Limpy walked forward. They stopped at six-gun range from each other.

"Are you going to kill Jigs?" Limpy asked.

"That don't need to concern you," said Slocum.

"That other bunch over yonder sure means to kill him."

"No reason for you to get killed along with him," Slocum said. "I see you've already lost one man."

"Well, my pards back there all say we ought to give him up. I hate to go back on my word to a man is all."

"Jigs is a worthless son of a bitch," Slocum said. "I don't think you need to worry about your word to him. Likely, he gave you a tall tale about why there was folks after him. Him and his partner murdered some of this bunch here." Slocum jerked his thumb back at Grimes's bunch. "It was a separate deal from why I'm after him."

"He never told us that," said Limpy. He looked back over his shoulder. "All right, boys," he said. "Bring Jigs on out."

The other two stood up tentatively. Jigs did not appear.

"Jigs," said one of them. "Come on. Get your ass up out of there."

They walked around poking through the tall grass, searching for Jigs.

"He was right here beside us," said the one with the wounded arm.

"Come on," said Grimes to his men. "Let's find him."

They all ran out into the grass. Grimes's men and the three ranch hands all stomped and kicked around in the grass.

"Goddamn it," said Grimes. "Find the son of a bitch."

Limpy turned around in a circle, his arms wide out to his sides indicating the sweeping prairie around him.

"Hell," he said, "he could be anywhere out here."

Slocum looked to his left. He saw the cookshack and the corral.

"I wonder," he said. Then he raised his voice to speak to Limpy. "Check your corral," he said.

16

"There's a horse and saddle missing," Limpy yelled from the corral.

"It figures," Slocum said. The others all ran over to join Limpy at the corral. Slocum strolled over, the last one to arrive. "You were protecting Jigs," he said to Limpy, "but when the going got tough, the little son of a bitch ran out and left you. You see what kind of a little chickenshit bastard he is?"

"If I ever see him again," Limpy said, "I'll kill him for you."

"If you all will back off some from that corral," Slocum said, "we might be able to tell something from the hoofprints."

"Ah, hell," said the wounded cowhand, "there's too many prints all over the place anyhow. We couldn't tell a damn thing."

"Wait a minute," said Limpy. "It's old Brownie that's missing."

"So what?" said the other cowhand.

"Brownie's got a shoe on his left front foot that's got a notch in it."

"I see the prints," Slocum said. "They're on top. He headed west across the prairie there."

"You're right," Limpy said.

"What's out that way?" Slocum asked.

"Nothing for quite a ways," Limpy said. "Except the boss might be coming back from that direction."

"Where's he been?" Grimes said.

Limpy hesitated. He realized that he and the other two were greatly outnumbered, but he wasn't at all sure that he should tell the truth about where Reb and the rest of the hands had gone. He wasn't sure about Slocum or about Grimes.

"Where the hell has he been?" said Grimes.

"Him and the rest of the boys went over into Colorado," Limpy finally said. "They had some business over there."

"Buying cattle?" Grimes asked.

"Well, no."

"Horses?"

"No."

"What then?" said Grimes. "Talk to me, you son of a bitch."

"All right," said Limpy. "They went to pull a job."

"Keep going," Grimes said, "or I'll blow your head off." He aimed his six-gun at Limpy's head and thumbed back the hammer.

"A gold shipment," Limpy said. "Being hauled in a special stage. They'll have it by now and be on their way back here."

"How come you ain't with them?" asked Grimes.

"Reb said that he needed some men to stick around here to keep an eye on things. He'll be mad as hell when he sees what happened to his house. He might kill us."

"You said Reb?" said Slocum. "Reb who?"

"Reb Gillian," Limpy answered. "This is his place here."

"Well, Goddamn," said Slocum.

"What is it, Slocum?" said Grimes. "You know this Gillian?"

"I know him all right," Slocum said. "He's a worthless bastard, too."

"How many men has Gillian got with him?" Grimes asked Limpy.

"He has eight of them and also that other fellow rode in. The one that done Jigs wrong. What the hell did they call him?"

"Sluice?" said Slocum.

"Yeah," said Limpy. "That's it. Sluice."

Slocum asked himself how lucky he could get. Sluice, Jigs, and Reb Gillian all in the same place. Well, nearly the same. Sluice and Reb were heading back this way, and Jigs was headed that way. They might run into each other. Then again, they might not. There was a lot of space out there.

"We going after them, Boss?" one of Grimes's men asked.

"Hell, yes," said Grimes. "Slocum? You coming?"

Slocum knew that Jigs was on his way west, but Sluice was the main one he wanted. Jigs would keep. And Sluice was on his way back to this place along with Reb Gillian. If he rode out with Grimes, or even without Grimes, there was always a chance he would ride right past them.

"You do what you want, Grimes," he said. "I'm waiting here."

Grimes glanced at Billy Pierce and Old Jan. "What about you two?" he asked.

"We stick with Slocum," Old Jan said.

"Yeah," Billy seconded.

"Suit yourselves," said Grimes. "Come on, boys. Let's get after them."

The Grimes bunch walked back to where they had left their horses and mounted up. Grimes led the way, and they all headed west. Slocum watched them until they disappeared.

"Slocum," said Old Jan. "You know, there's a chance they might catch up with Jigs. They might even run across Sluice and them."

"Let them," said Slocum. He pulled a cigar out of his pocket and stuck it between his lips. "If they find Jigs, they'll kill him. I don't give a shit about that." He found a match and struck it against the corral. Holding the flame against the end of his cigar, he puffed until he had it going. Whiffs of blue smoke rode up above his head.

"And if they run across Sluice and that bunch?" Old Jan asked.

"Sluice and Red and that bunch will wipe them out," Slocum said. "Grimes and his gang might kill a few of Reb's outfit before they all bite the dust. Then Reb and Sluice and the others will come back here, just like they planned. And that'll be all right, too."

Sheriff Holmes and an eight-man posse were examining the scene of the robbery. They had gathered all the bodies and loaded them into the coach. The sheriff ordered one of the men to drive the coach back to the nearest town and report what they had found. Holmes was sick at what had happened. The special guards had all been friends of his. The coach rumbled off down the road with its grisly cargo, and Holmes stood in the middle of the road and watched it go. He now had seven men. He also had a special reason to capture or kill these outlaws.

"Sheriff," said one of the men. "They rode off east across the prairie. I found their tracks."

"All right," said Holmes. "Mount up. Let's get after them."

The men who were on foot mounted their horses, and Holmes led the posse after the outlaws. They all rode with grim and determined faces.

Slocum thought about killing Limpy and his two pals. They rode for Reb Gillian, and so did Sluice. They had to be worthless shits. But they had done nothing to Slocum, nor had they done anything he was witness to or had heard about. He had Billy and Old Jan take their weapons from them. They could live, at least for the time being. He searched the ground for the highest spot, and sent Billy to go out and watch the west for any sign of the returning band of outlaws. Then he took Old Jan and the three Gillian men into the cookshack. There was plenty of food in there and coffee, and he even found some bottles of good whiskey.

Slocum felt the need for a good drunk, and he did not think that anyone would be showing up any time soon. He took down one of the bottles and uncorked it. He had a good drink and offered the bottle to Old Jan. Old Jan refused it, so Slocum had another pull on the bottle. The whiskey was smooth. At the same time, it burned his throat on the way down and burned his belly when it hit bottom. Limpy and his two partners sat across the room from Slocum. They watched him drink for a while, licking their lips. At last, one of them spoke.

"Say, Slocum," he said, "can we have a drink?"

"Why not?" Slocum said. He gestured toward the shelf that held the bottles. "Get a bottle. But keep your seats over there."

"Sure," said the man. "Thanks."

He got a bottle and returned to his seat. Uncorking the bottle, he took a drink and passed it along to Limpy. Limpy drank and handed it to the third man. Slocum had another drink from his bottle. Soon he felt a bit woozy. He was glad that Old Jan had refused to drink.

"Jan," he said. "Keep your eyes on those bastards. I'll likely pass out before long."

"Don't worry, Slocum. I'm watching them like a cat watches a mouse."

In a few more minutes, Slocum's prediction came true. He slumped forward onto the table and drifted into a worry-free unconsciousness. Old Jan sat up watching the three men across the room drink themselves into the same kind of stupor. He waited until they were passed out or nearly so, then tied their hands behind their backs and went out to relieve Billy Pierce.

Grimes and his six men topped a rise, and they saw the outlaws riding toward them.

"There they are," he said.

"About ten of them," said one of the men. "We're outnumbered."

"Get down behind this knoll," said Grimes, "and open fire

with your rifles as soon as you can get a good shot. We'll change the odds soon."

The men rode back down the knoll and dismounted, clambering back to the top and falling flat on their bellies and readying their rifles. They waited as the outlaw gang drew closer. Luckily, they had not been spotted.

Gillian and Sluice rode side by side, with another man riding to each side. The rest brought up the rear. Suddenly, unexpected gunshots rang out. Sluice felt a bullet tear his right ear. He yelped and flung himself off his horse in a flash and onto his belly in the dirt. Ignoring the bleeding ear, he jerked loose his six-gun and looked for a target. Gillian had hit the dirt just a split second before, but he had jerked out his rifle before falling. The others behind them also fell to the ground, but neither Sluice nor Gillian had any idea how many of them fell of their own accord or were dropped by bullets. The horses, with the bags of gold on their backs, ran wild.

It did not take the Gillian gang long to locate their targets and start returning fire. The fight did not last long. In spite of their slight advantage of higher ground and surprise, Grimes's men were easily overwhelmed. Grimes found himself left with one man. The others were dead. He could see that the horses of his enemies were scattered. His own were still bunched up behind them. He turned to his sole surviving underling and said, "Let's get the hell out of here." They crept backward a short distance, then got up and ran for their horses. Initially, they raced back east, but as soon as they got a safe distance away, they turned north. They left five horses behind, with the bodies of five of their men.

"They're getting away," said Sluice, standing up.

"Let them go," said Gillian. "We won't see them again."

"I'd sure like to know who the hell they were," Sluice said.

"What difference does it make? We cut them to pieces."

"We didn't come out so good ourselves," said a voice behind them. Sluice and Gillian both turned around to look.

There were three men standing behind them. The rest were lying dead.

"Catch up the horses," said Gillian. "All of them. They're all carrying gold."

Jigs had been riding on a more or less parallel path to that of Grimes and his men. He was somewhat north of them and a little farther west, but not so far that he did not hear the shots. He wondered what was going on. Then he figured that the gang Sluice was riding with would be coming back this way, and it was quite possible that Grimes and Slocum and all those might be after him. They might have run into each other. He thought about riding away as fast as he could, but his curiosity got the better of him. He wondered who was killed. It wouldn't bother him at all if anyone on either side got killed, but he particularly hoped that at least Sluice and Grimes were dead. He would piss on their bodies. He turned his horse and rode toward where the shots seemed to have come from. As he rode along, he spied a small hill just off to his left. He made for it and rode to the top. There he dismounted and made sure that his horse was out of sight. Then he found a spot behind a rock and snugged down behind it.

He did not have to wait long. Two riders were headed his way. He watched anxiously as they drew closer. He wished that he had a rifle, but all he had was his six-gun. He drew it out and held it ready. The riders came closer. He waited a little longer, and then he recognized them. Grimes and one of the men who had beat on him. His heart pounded with anxiety. His palms began to sweat. He was overwhelmed with a desire to kill. They came closer. Jigs eased himself down lower on the side of the hill. He moved carefully. He did not want to give himself away.

The riders were moving in a direction that would take them close to the hill. Jigs could hardly stand the wait. Then he could not believe his good fortune. They stopped their horses right at the base of the hill and dismounted. Grimes sat down on a small boulder, the other man on the ground. Jigs continued easing himself down. He had a good shot. He started to raise his gun to shoot, but the men below started to talk. He waited to hear what they would say.

"So what do we do from here, Boss?" said the one man.

"We don't quit," said Grimes. "We ride back to Bascomb and get some more men. I mean to kill Jigs and Sluice. This little setback ain't going to stop me."

"They might be anywhere by the time we get there and back," the man said.

"We'll find them," Grimes said. "The only thing that worries me is that Slocum will get Sluice before I do. Sluice and those others are headed right back for the ranch, and he's waiting there for them."

"Boss?" said the man.

"What?"

"Did you see them bags on their horses?"

"Bags? What are you talking about, Rimes?"

"It looked to me like every one of their horses was packing two heavy bags hanging from the saddle horn. The only thing I can think of they might have been full of is gold."

"How can you tell that from looking at a bag?"

"They went out on a job to steal some gold according to that Limpy fellow," said Rimes. "Each horse was packing two bags. Heavy-looking bags. It had to be the gold."

"I bet you're right," said Grimes. "We'll have to hurry back to Bascomb. We need to get back to that bunch while they've still got it on them. Come on."

Both men stood up, and Jigs fired. His bullet hit Rimes in the chest, knocking him back into his horse. Grimes turned and went for his gun, but Jigs fired again. This time he hit Grimes in the right shoulder, causing him to drop his six-gun and stagger. Jigs got up from behind his boulder and started down the hillside, still holding his gun on Grimes.

"Well, now," he said, "Mr. Grimes, you slimy no-good piece of snake shit. It looks like now the shoe's on the other foot, don't it? I been waiting for this a long time now. I been longing for it."

"Go ahead and shoot, you little chickenshit," said Grimes.

"Oh, no," said Jigs. "I ain't in no hurry. I mean to enjoy this. I'm thinking about when you had all them men beat up on me. All at once. Hitting me and kicking me. And me with my nose shot off and hurting. They broke my ribs. Hurt me all over. I couldn't even set on a horse, so they tied me to the saddle. Sent the horse running out of town, with me hurt and starving. I cried, Grimes. I was hurt so bad, I cried. I wouldn't tell that to nobody, but I'm telling it to you on account of I'm fixing to kill you, so it don't matter if you know about it. You're dead."

"Fuck you," said Grimes.

"Fuck you, too," said Jigs, and he shot Grimes in the left kneecap. Grimes yelled in pain and grabbed his knee, almost falling over.

"Go on and kill me," said Grimes.

"Don't be in such a hurry," said Jigs. He shot Grimes's other knee, and Grimes, screaming with pain, dropped to the ground. Jigs holstered his six-gun. "Come to think of it," he said, "I don't believe I'll kill you at all." He slid a long skinning knife out of a sheath on his belt and stepped forward. He took hold of Grimes's left ear and pulled, then sliced with the knife. Grimes screamed again. Jigs did the same thing to the other ear. He tossed the ears off to the side. "I think I'll just leave you here to bleed yourself to death."

17

Sluice, Gillian, and the remaining three riders of the old Gillian gang were busy chasing horses for some time. They caught enough for themselves, but there were still others running loose. The horses were not important, but each horse was carrying two bags of gold. Neither Sluice nor Gillian was willing to let that go. They kept chasing the spooked animals. The three extra hands at last caught all but one. No one could get close to it. Sluice pulled out his rifle and cranked a shell into the chamber.

"I'll get the goddamned thing," he said.

He raised the rifle to his shoulder and took aim. He pulled the trigger, sending a bullet smashing into the horse and dropping it instantly. They rode to get the gold. Soon, they had all the gold loaded on a couple of extra horses, and they started for the ranch. They had not gone far, though, when Holmes and his posse appeared on the horizon.

"Look," said Sluice. "Who the hell is that?"

Gillian looked back over his shoulder.

"It looks like a damned posse to me," he said. He looked ahead again at a small outcropping slightly to their left. "Head in there," he said, "and use your rifles."

They rode for cover, dismounted, and secured the horses. All five men readied their rifles and waited for the posse to come into range. Then five rifles sounded and five members of the posse dropped from their saddles. The sheriff and the two remaining posse members all dismounted and fell flat to the ground. Their frightened horses scattered.

"Sheriff," said one, "we're like sitting ducks here."

"Shut up and shoot back," Holmes said.

"My rifle's still in the boot," said the man.

"Mine, too," said the other man. "They're out of six-gun range."

"Then just keep on eating dirt," Holmes said.

Back behind his cover, Gillian said to Sluice and the others, "They've lost their horses. Let's get out of here."

They mounted up and gathered the reins of the extra horses. Then they resumed their ride to the ranch. Holmes and his men heard them ride away. They stood up and looked around for their horses. Most of them had not gone far. In an hour or so, they had them all.

"Let's get back on their trail," Holmes said.

"I'm heading home," said one man.

The other man agreed.

"What the hell's wrong with you?" Holmes said. "They've killed our friends. They have all that gold. You want to let them get away?"

"There ain't as many of us as what started out," said one man. "And we've rode farther away from home than what we expected."

"What the hell did you expect?" said Holmes. "Did you expect a guarantee that we'd catch up with them in a mile? Or two? Did you expect them to all lay down their weapons when they saw us coming?"

"You can say anything you want to," said one man. "We're leaving."

"All right," said Holmes. "All right then. At least load up these bodies and take them along with you."

"Take them along with us? What are you going to do?"

"I'm keeping after those goddamned outlaws," said the sheriff.

Jigs was feeling like hot shit. He had finally encountered Grimes, one of the men he most wanted revenge on, and he had left him in miserable condition to die alone and painfully, his kneecaps shot and his ears cut off. Perhaps coyotes or buzzards would even go to work on him before he was quite dead. Jigs laughed out loud at that new thought. He was riding in a southeasterly direction, thinking that he might encounter Sluice and those others along the way. If he could kill Sluice, he would be satisfied.

He was surprised when he came across a lone rider who seemed to be following someone. He laid back to stay out of sight, but he dogged the trail of the lone rider. At one point, the lone rider stopped and dismounted, apparently taking a break, resting his horse. The man rolled himself a smoke and lit it, and as he turned to sit down on the ground, the sun glinted on his chest. A badge, Jigs thought. It was a lawman. Could he be after Sluice and the rest of that gang for stealing the gold? He decided to stay on the trail of this lone lawman.

When Gillian, Sluice, and the other three men drew close to the ranch house, Gillian saw smoke. It wasn't much smoke, not like a fire raging. It was more like smoke from the smoldering remains of a fire. It was enough smoke, though, to worry Gillian.

"It looks like it's coming from my house," he said, "or close to it. Let's ease up on it."

They rode slower, and when they finally came in view, Gillian could see that his house was gone. It had burned.

"Damn it," he said. "What the hell did Limpy and them do?"

He spurred his horse to hurry on to his house, or what remained of it, but a shout from Sluice stopped him.

"Hold it, Reb," Sluice called out.

Gillian hauled back on the reins of his mount and turned in the saddle.

"What?" he snapped. "What?"

"You might be riding into something you don't want to ride into," said Sluice. "Anyone got some glasses?"

One of the three outlaws reached into his saddlebags and pulled out a set of binoculars, holding them out to Sluice. Impatient, Gillian rode back and waited while Sluice zeroed in on the burned house and then the cookshack and the corral. He spotted the Appaloosa right away.

"Goddamn," he said.

"What?" said Gillian. Sluice held the glasses toward Gillian.

"Take a look," he said. "I killed a man a while back who was riding a spotty-ass horse like that. He was on my trail. Out to get me."

Gillian located the horse. "It don't belong in my corral," he said. "You say you killed the man?"

"I did."

"You shoot him from a distance or get him up close?"

"He fell off the edge of the road. I went to look, but I couldn't even find the body."

"Yeah? Well, if you didn't actual see him dead, you might have just thought you killed him."

Sluice sat for a moment, thoughtful. He scratched his beard. "Damn," he said. "You could be right about that."

Gillian raised the glasses again just as Old Jan walked out of the cookshack. "There's a stranger down there all right," he said. He swung the glasses back to the corral and looked closer. "There's more horses there that ain't mine," he said. "I'd say there's someone down there laying for us."

"So what are we going to do?" Sluice asked. "Do we ride in shooting?"

"We don't know how many of them are in there," Gillian said. "They're holed up in the cookshack, and we'd be out in the open. No. I say let's ride out."

"Leave your ranch?"

"We got enough gold here to buy ten ranches like that, or more. Anything worth a damn was in the house anyhow."

"All right," said Sluice. "Where will we go?"

"That way," said Gillian, pointing northwest. "A little mining town out there in the foothills called Devil's Gap. We'll go there."

He turned his horse and led the way with Sluice and the other three following. Without knowing it, of course, they rode in the path of Sheriff Holmes as he rode toward the ranch house with Jigs still riding on his trail.

It was sometime later when Sheriff Holmes rode up to the cookshack. Slocum heard him coming and went outside. Pretty soon Billy and Old Jan joined him. "Just one rider," said Old Jan. "It can't be Gillian or Sluice."

"Not hardly," said Slocum.

They waited until Holmes pulled up just a few feet away.

"Howdy," said Holmes.

"Howdy," said Old Jan.

"You're a lawman," said Slocum.

"That's right. I was trailing a gang of outlaws. They were headed this way, but I lost their trail a ways back. I don't suppose you've seen any strangers coming through here."

"No," said Slocum, "but we've been expecting a bunch. Might be the same ones. Why don't you get down? Come inside and have some grub."

"Thanks," said Holmes. "I will."

Inside the cookshack, Holmes stopped, a surprised look on his face.

"Oh," said Slocum. "Those three hog-tied over there are part of that outlaw bunch we're waiting for. The man that owns this ranch is named Reb Gillian. He took his whole crew somewhere west to rob a gold shipment. Left four men here to guard his ranch. These three are left."

"Then it is the same bunch," Holmes said. "They stopped the stagecoach. Killed the driver and all of the guards and got away with the gold. What's your interest in them?"

Slocum poured Holmes a cup of coffee and asked Old Jan to fetch him some food. He then told the tale of Trent Brady's murder and the ambush that laid him up and the killing of Charlie Gourd. He told Holmes about Jigs and about Grimes and his men. Old Jan put a plate of hot food in front of Holmes, and the sheriff started to dig in.

"How come you went to strike out after a gang that size by yourself?" Slocum asked.

"I had a posse when I left," Holmes said. "The gang waylaid us. Killed several of my men. The rest quit on me and headed for home."

"So you kept on by yourself?"

"Those guards were friends of mine," Holmes said. "And the members of my posse that the gang killed."

"I see," Slocum said.

"Not everything you don't," said Holmes. "I'm out of my jurisdiction now. I'm just a private citizen."

"Well, then," Slocum said, "you ought to put away that star."

The sheriff looked down at the badge on his breast. "I reckon you're right," he said, and he pulled off the star and tucked it into a pocket. He continued eating. "So you think that bunch is coming back here?" he said.

"We been counting on it," said Slocum. "It's Gillian's place. I can't think why he'd go anyplace else."

"Smoke's still rising up from where the house used to be," said Holmes. "I noticed it back a ways. Gillian will see it, too. It might scare him off."

"You're right," said Slocum. "And you were behind him. Right?"

"That's right."

"Then he should've got here already."

"If he was coming here."

"We'd better ride your back trail," said Slocum. "See if we can pick up anything."

"Let's go then," said Holmes, standing up to leave.

"You need a fresh horse?"

"I'd take one."

They went back outside and saddled a horse for Holmes as well as Slocum's Appaloosa.

"You want me and Old Jan to ride along with you?" Billy asked as Slocum and Holmes mounted up.

"No," said Slocum. "Wait here. We'll be back."

They rode out in the direction Holmes had come from. They rode slowly, looking for any sign of other riders. After a few minutes, Holmes said, "Right about here is where I spotted the smoke." They stopped and looked back. From their location, the smoke was just visible.

"If Gillian spotted it, too," Slocum said, "he'd have been close to here. Let's ride north."

They turned their horses and rode slowly, watching the ground. They got some distance north and lost sight of the smoke, so they turned west a short distance and then headed south again, still riding slowly.

"There," said Slocum. "Look there."

"Someone rode hard toward the ranch, stopped, turned, and rode back," said Holmes.

"That's how I read it," said Slocum.

They followed the tracks back to where they joined up with the tracks of several other horses.

"Looks like they stood here for a bit," Slocum said.

"They spotted the smoke and sat and talked about what to do," Holmes said.

"Then they decided to hightail it out of here," Slocum said. "They're going back west."

"Kind of northwest," Holmes said.

"Yeah."

"You riding after them?"

"Not till morning," Slocum said. "Right now, I'll go back to the cookshack. We'll pack for the trail, and head out with first light in the morning. You're welcome to ride along if you like."

"Thanks," said Holmes. "I'll take you up on that."

Slocum and Holmes rode back to the corral, unsaddled their horses, and turned them loose inside the fence. Slocum made sure there was food and water for them. Old Jan and Billy came walking up.

"What did you find out there?" Billy asked.

"We found their trail," said Slocum. "We're going after them first thing in the morning."

"I'll pack up any food that'll keep on the trail," said Old Jan. "Some plates and cups."

"Yeah," said Slocum. "All the ammunition you can find, and what's left of the whiskey."

"You notice those hoofprints, Slocum?" Holmes said.

"Yeah. I'd say the horses were all packing gold."

"That's what I say."

"It'll slow them down some," said Slocum.

"Yeah, but they got a good start on us. They might make Devil's Gap before we catch up with them."

"Devil's Gap?" Slocum said.

"It's a mining town in the foothills west of here," said Holmes. "Small place. No sheriff or any kind of lawman."

"No law?"

"Just a miners' court," said Holmes.

"Say, Slocum," said Billy.

"Yeah?"

"What are we going to do about them three we got tied up inside?"

"We might leave them to starve," Slocum said.

"We can't do that," said Old Jan.

Slocum turned and walked back into the shack. He looked at Limpy and the other two.

"Your boss ran out on you," he said.

"I ain't surprised," said Limpy. "Not after what we learned about that goddamned Sluice. And they're pards."

"What'll you do if we turn you loose?"

"Head for Texas," said Limpy.

"Good," said Slocum. "That sounds to me like a damn good idea."

18

Reb Gillian, Sluice, and their three gunhands approached Devil's Gap about the middle of the day on a sunny day. They halted a little above the town while Gillian studied it.

"What're you waiting for, Reb?" said Sluice.

"That's a rough town down there," Gillian said. "It might be kind of stupid riding down there with all this gold on these horses."

"Oh," said Sluice. "Yeah. I guess you're right about that. So what'll we do?"

Reb dismounted and looked around. There was a small shack up against a hillside. It seemed to be deserted. Reb jerked his thumb toward it. "Homer," he said, "you boys check that out."

The three men rode over to the shack and dismounted. Homer led them into the shack. In a minute, Homer came back out. He walked around to the side of the house. Then he walked around to the other side. There was a small corral with a couple of busted rails. Homer remounted his horse and rode back over to where Gillian stood waiting. The other two gunnies followed him.

"Well?" said Reb.

"Place is deserted," said Homer. "Ain't no one been in there for some time, I'd say."

"All right," said Reb. "We're taking it over. First thing, let's unload all this gold into the house. Then put the horses in the corral."

The men all set to work. Gillian found some loose floorboards and pulled them up. He had the men stash the gold under the floor and replace the boards, although he hauled out a couple of handfuls of coins first and put them in his pocket. The men unloaded the horses and put them in the corral. Gillian had the men leave his horse and Sluice's saddled. When they were all done, he said, "You three stay here and guard this place. Look around for some water and fill that old trough out in the corral. Me and Sluice is going into town to check things out. We'll bring back some oats for the horses."

"How about some fresh grub?" asked one of the men.

"We'll bring it," said Gillian.

"And some whiskey," said Homer.

"That, too," Gillian said. "All right, Sluice. Let's go look it over."

They mounted up and headed for Devil's Gap. Homer and the other two stood and watched them go. Then Homer said, "Well, let's go find some water."

"I seen a pump over by the corral," said one.

"Oh, yeah?" said Homer. "Let's check it out and see if it still works."

They found an old bucket and the pump worked. It wasn't long before they had the trough filled and the horses were drinking. They dug some hardtack and jerky out of their packs and sat down outside in front of the shack to eat.

"Any idea how long they'll be gone?" said one.

"Hell, Bobtail," said Homer, "they'll be gone a while. Don't worry about it."

"I'd sure like to have some good grub," Bobtail said.

"Whiskey," said the third man.

"I'm with you, Carlos," said Homer. "But we'll just have to wait."

"Say," Bobtail said. "Why should we hang around here?"

"What do you mean?" Homer asked.

"Just this," said Bobtail. "I don't know what the hell is in this fucking dirty little town for us. We've already got enough gold to keep us living in style for the rest of our lives."

"Go on," said Carlos.

"I say let's take two bags of that stuff and head for California. San Francisco maybe. We can live like kings, and no one would ever find us there."

"I don't like Californee," said Homer. "I was out there once before. They're still looking for me, I reckon."

"Well, then, St. Louee, or maybe New Orleans," Bobtail said.

"I've always wanted to see New Orleans," said Carlos.

"If we take off from here with some of that gold," Homer said, "Reb's really going to be pissed off at us."

"You think he'll come after us?" Bobtail asked.

"He might," said Carlos.

"We won't be taking no more than our share," said Bobtail.

"Yeah, but taking it and running off behind his back is what will piss him off," said Homer.

"I'm sure getting tired of hardtack and jerky," Carlos said. "There's fancy food in New Orleans."

"And plenty of whiskey," said Bobtail.

"Well," said Homer, "what do you say?"

"I say we take a bag each," said Carlos. "That still leaves them two with plenty. They find out how much we left for them, they ought to be glad we left them so much. They shouldn't even bother following us."

"They'll follow us all right," said Homer. "Our only chance will be to ride hard and ride fast and cover our trail. And the sooner we get started, the better."

Homer and Bobtail went out to saddle the horses while Carlos pulled up the floorboards and hauled out three bags of gold. They poured the gold into their saddlebags, half a bag in each side. They did think to replace the floorboards before taking off, but soon, they were headed southeast.

Out on the prairie, Sheriff Holmes, Slocum, Old Jan, and Billy Pierce were riding toward Devil's Gap. They did not know it, but Jigs was on their trail not far behind. They were riding along at a leisurely pace to save the horses.

"How much longer do you reckon it is to Devil's Gap?" Slocum asked.

"I'd say we have another half day's ride," Holmes said.

"You think they'll still be there?" Billy asked.

"There ain't no other place for them to go up this way," Holmes said. "They'll be there all right."

Just at that moment, three riders topped a slight rise ahead of them. They did not recognize the riders. They could have been any passing strangers, but one of the riders did recognize Holmes.

"Hey," shouted Homer. "It's that goddamned sheriff."

He jerked out his six-gun and fired a wild shot. Slocum dismounted quickly, dragging his Winchester with him. He dropped to the ground on his stomach. Billy, Old Jan, and the sheriff were not far behind him. The three outlaws did the same. No one had a good, clear shot, but that did not stop them from shooting. A bullet hit the ground a couple of feet in front of Slocum's face. He scooted back a little farther. Billy Pierce fired a shot at the outlaws, but it missed its mark. Old Jan was waiting for a good shot. The sheriff was waiting, too, while he watched the outlaws' horses running loose back behind them. He was thinking that at least some of the gold had to be on those horses.

Across the way, Bobtail said to Homer, "I think if I can get a little closer, I can get a shot at one of them."

"There's no cover up there," Homer said.

"If I just scoot myself," Bobtail said, "I think I can do it."

"You'd be taking a chance," Homer said.

"It's better than just laying here in this Mexican stand-off," Bobtail said, and he started to scooch himself forward. A shot from the other side came close to him and made him stop. Homer looked back behind him at the loose horses. He nudged Carlos.

"What?" Carlos said.

"Let Bobtail get up a little bit farther," said Homer, "and then let's grab our horses and get the hell out of here."

"That's a dirty trick," said Carlos.

"It's better than getting killed out here, ain't it?"

Carlos looked forward to where Bobtail was still scooting forward. He looked back at Homer. "Say when," he said.

Homer waited a little longer while Bobtail moved on still farther. Then he said, "Let's go."

Homer shoved himself backward staying on his belly, and Carlos followed his example. When they were back down the slope a ways, Homer stood up in a crouch and ran for his horse. Carlos did the same. They reached the horses and mounted up quickly, turning them to ride south. Holmes saw them, and snapped off a shot from his Henry rifle. He missed, but Bobtail saw him shoot and twisted his head to see what the sheriff had shot at. He saw Homer and Carlos riding away. He turned and sat up, aiming his rifle.

"You sons of bitches," he shouted, and he fired, his bullet catching Carlos in the small of the back. Carlos flung his arms up and fell backward over the horse's rump, turning a flip and landing hard on his face and stomach.

Billy Pierce stood up and fired at Bobtail, catching him between the shoulder blades. Bobtail fell forward at first, then rocked back and sprawled out on the ground. Homer was racing away as fast as he could go.

Slocum and the rest mounted up and rode toward the bodies. Billy checked Bobtail and found that he was dead. Old Jan rode on to where Carlos had fallen. He, too, was done for. Holmes caught up the first horse he came to and checked the saddlebags.

"They're full of the stolen gold," he yelled. "Grab that other one over there."

Old Jan went after the last loose horse, while Slocum lit out after Homer.

Looking over his shoulder, Homer saw that he was being chased. This was not the way he had planned it. He had figured that Bobtail would keep them busy long enough for him and Carlos to get safely away, but the fool had turned and fired at his own buddies. Goddamn him to hell. Homer lashed at his horse, but it was weighted down with gold, and it likely would not have been a match for the big Appaloosa following him anyway. He saw his opportunity and swung around behind a large boulder, where he dismounted with his rifle. He took aim over the boulder and snapped off a shot at Slocum. It came close. Slocum pulled off behind some brush and dismounted with his Winchester. He could see where Homer was hidden.

Homer's horse had wandered out into the open, and Slocum took careful aim and fired a shot. His bullet tore the saddlebag on the horse's right side. The horse nickered and reared a bit, but it did not run. Slocum aimed a second time. This time, his shot tore the bag open and gold coins started to pour out onto the ground. From his spot behind the boulder, Homer could see the coins falling.

"Hey," he yelled. "Goddamn it."

He fired a shot in Slocum's general direction, then ran out to his horse. He first tried to stop the flow of the coins, then decided that he was in Slocum's line of fire. He grabbed the reins and started pulling the horse behind the boulder. His first thought was that if he could kill the son of a bitch, he would pick up the fallen coins. Then he decided against that. He still had one bag filled. That would be enough. There were those other men back there, and they would surely be coming up here soon. He fired another shot close to where he figured Slocum was hiding.

But Slocum was not there. He had begun working his way through the brush, heading for a location on a line from where Homer was behind his boulder. Homer fired again. He waited. He got no reaction of any kind to his shot. He looked around in desperation. Damn it, he thought. Where is he? Where is the bastard? Just then he heard a voice, close.

"Hey, you," it said.

He turned quickly and saw Slocum standing just across the way facing him. There was nothing between them. Each man had a clear shot. Homer hesitated. Then he swung his rifle around. Slocum's Colt barked, and a bullet tore into Homer's chest. He felt the impact. He felt it burn its way into him. His fingers grew limp and he dropped his rifle. He looked down at the growing red splotch on his chest, and then he pitched forward dead.

Shortly, the other men joined Slocum. They gathered up the spilt money and stuffed it into the other saddlebags.

"There are only the two of them now," said Holmes. "They don't know it, but they'll be waiting for us in Devil's Gap."

Jigs watched it all happen from a safe spot some distance away. When he finally saw Slocum and the others riding away, he carefully made his way down to the scene of the recent conflict. The first thing he came across was the body of Bobtail. He took all the guns and ammunition and what little cash he found on it. He moved on to where Carlos had fallen and did the same to him. He had four new guns and about six dollars. Leading his horse, he made his way to where Slocum had encountered Homer, and he found Homer's body. Again, he got the guns and the money. He now had a little over ten dollars, six new guns, and three belts of ammunition. He was disappointed. He had hoped to find more cash. Maybe the goddamned sheriff and those others had beaten him to it. He could not figure out why they had left the ten dollars, though. He was just turning, starting to walk back to his horse, when he spotted a gold coin on the ground. His eyes lit up. He ran to it and picked it up. He held it close to his face. It had to be a part of the gold that Gillian and Sluice and the others had gone after.

So the sheriff and those others had it now. They had ridden on with all the horses of the three men they had killed. The gold had to be on those horses. He decided that he would follow it. He had no idea what he would do when he caught up with them, but he could not ride away from all that gold. He had to go after them. He tucked the gold coin in his pocket with the ten dollars or so he had gotten off the three dead bodies, mounted his horse, and continued following the sheriff and the others.

They had said they were going to Texas, but Limpy and his two pards got to thinking about all the gold that Gillian would have, and they agreed that they were owed a share. They packed for a long ride and started after the sheriff and the others. They were well behind, so they rode along at a good clip. Each of them also had a full bottle of whiskey in his saddlebags. As they rode along, one of the men pulled out his bottle and uncorked it as he rode. He took a good, long swig.

"Hey, Bo," said Limpy. "You don't want to go getting drunk in the saddle. You're liable to fall off somewhere along the way."

"Ah, that ain't going to happen," said Bo, and he took another drink.

The third man was watching, and he was easily persuaded. He pulled out his bottle and joined Bo in his revelry. They rode on awhile before Limpy said, "Aw, hell," and he brought out his own and joined them. Soon, they started singing bawdy songs out of tune in gravelly voices. They began rocking and swaying in their saddles. They were following a winding and narrow trail leading generally northwest, and for a short distance there were trees and brush on each side. Bo tipped his bottle back and had another drink. He lost his grip and dropped the bottle. He swayed dizzily and fell off to one side. He hung on to the saddle horn with one hand, and his head was almost dragging in the dirt.

"Hey, Limpy," said the third man. "Look at ole Bo." Then he laughed out loud. Limpy turned to look, and he, too, started to laugh. Just then, Bo lost his grip and toppled to the ground.

"Well," said the other man, "you want to stop for him or ride on and leave his drunk ass here?"

19

The prairie between the Gillian ranch and the road to Devil's Gap in the foothills of the mountains was wide open, but it was crossed by a few well-worn paths or trails. The result was that any travelers across the prairie would likely either run into one another or at least cross one another's paths. Slocum, Holmes, Billy, and Old Jan were out ahead of everyone else, but Jigs was about to come up on Limpy and his two buddies, who had stopped to camp because of drunkenness.

At their rough campsite, Limpy and one man sat up drinking beside a campfire. Bo was already passed out. The sun was down, and the night was getting cold. Limpy said to the other man, "Bernie?"

"Whut?" Bernie answered.

"It's getting a little bit of a chill in the air, ain't it?"

"Yeah. It is."

"You reckon we ought to drag ole Bo up closer to the fire?"

"Well," said Bernie, "I reckon it might do him a little good."

"Might keep him from getting a harmful chill overnight," said Limpy.

"Yeah," said Bernie, taking another pull on his bottle. "It might do that."

Limpy took another slug from his bottle. He set the bottle down and dug into his shirt pocket for the makings of a cigarette. Then he started to roll himself a smoke. Finishing the job, he poked the cigarette between his lips, picked up a burning stick from the fire, and lit his smoke. Bernie watched him exhale and said, "Hey. Let me have some of that." Limpy handed the makings to Bernie. Soon both men were smoking and drinking together. Bo started to snore and snort.

"We really ought to drag him closer to the fire," said Limpy.

Jigs was still riding, but he was thinking about stopping somewhere for the night. He figured that the ground was a little tricky for night riding. He was still thinking about all that gold. Sluice and Gillian had to have it. Most of it anyhow. That goddamned sheriff and his cohorts had some of it. They had the share that those three owlhoots of Gillian's had run off with. He was thinking so hard about the gold and how he would get it away from one bunch or the other that his head was starting to hurt. He had never had to do too much thinking for himself. Someone else had always done it for him. Most recently, it had been Sluice, but Sluice had double-crossed him twice. Left him to get caught or killed. Now he had to think for himself. The other way had not worked out so well. He wanted to get even with Sluice. And he wanted that gold. Suddenly, he hauled back on the reins and stopped his horse. He saw the light from a fire ahead right on the trail he was riding.

He began easing forward slowly, keeping as quiet as he could. Drawing closer, he could see that two men were sitting around the fire. He moved in yet closer, and he drew his six-gun and cocked it. He moved yet closer. He stopped again. "Hey, you in the camp," he called out. Limpy and Bernie each came to their feet in a hurry and hauled out their six-guns, squinting out into the darkness, looking for their unexpected visitor. Limpy staggered a bit from his drunkenness.

"Who the hell are you?" he called out.

Limpy was standing on the other side of the fire, and the light glimmered over his face. Jigs recognized him.

"Limpy," he said. "By God. I'm glad to see you. This here is Jigs. Can I ride on in?"

"Jigs?" said Limpy. "You alone?"

"Hell, yeah. It's just me."

"Well, shit," said Limpy. "Come on in."

The two gunnies holstered their weapons as Jigs came into view. He dismounted, putting his horse with the other three. Turning to face Limpy and Bernie, he noticed a third man laid out on the ground.

"Who the hell is that?" he said.

"That's Bo," said Limpy. "Remember him? He's passed out."

"Oh, yeah," said Jigs. "I recall Bo."

"And Bernie here."

"Sure. How you doing, Bernie?"

"I'm all right," Bernie said.

"But what about you?" Limpy said to Jigs. "When you disappeared during that gun battle, we never knew what come of you."

"Well," said Jigs, "I hope you don't think I run out on you. I just knowed that fucking Grimes was after me, so I got the hell out of there. I figured Grimes and them would stop fighting if I was gone. I was right, wasn't I?"

"Yeah," said Limpy. "The way things turned out, I reckon you was. Sit down and have a drink."

Jigs moved up to the fire and sat down. Limpy passed his bottle to him. Jigs had a good, long drink before he gave it back.

"Thanks, Limpy," he said. "That sure was good. Just what I needed. Say. I'm glad I run across you boys."

"Yeah?"

"You know all that gold that Gillian and Sluice and them went after?"

"Yeah," said Limpy, somewhat cautiously.

"Well, I'm on its trail. It seems they got it all right. Then they got back to the ranch and seen the place all burned up.

They turned around and headed back this way. They run into a sheriff and had a fight. Seems the posse all got wiped out, all but the sheriff. It seems like Gillian and Sluice is the only ones left. There was three others with part of the gold, but the sheriff and them three that was after me and Sluice got them, and they got that part of the gold, too. So now there's two bunches of them out there, each one with part of the gold. I don't rightly care which ones I catch up with. Or both."

Limpy took another drink and handed the bottle back to Jigs. "Funny thing," he said, "but we kind of had the same idea. Only, you got more information than what we had."

"What do you say we team up?" Jigs asked.

"I say you got a pretty good idea there, pard."

Gillian and Sluice returned to the shack outside of Devil's Gap. They went to the corral to put up their horses, and right away noticed the missing horses.

"What the fuck?" said Gillian.

They rushed into the shack and looked around quickly. There was, of course, no sign of Homer and the other two men. Gillian rushed to the loose floorboards and jerked them up. He pulled out sacks of gold and counted them.

"The chickenshits took off with some of the gold," he said.

"We going after them?" Sluice asked.

Gillian walked slowly to the table. He pulled out a chair and sat down heavily. He heaved a sigh. "Hell," he said, "I guess not. They didn't take no more than their share. I reckon we can let them go with it. Fuck them. We don't need them nohow. You and me will just get ourselves set up here in Devil's Gap."

"What if we ever run into them three again?" Sluice said.

"If that happens," said Gillian, "we'll kill them."

Slocum and the others stopped for the night. Holmes told them that they were very close to Devil's Gap. They all agreed that Sluice and Gillian and the rest of the stolen gold would be there. It had been a long ride for Slocum, Billy, and Old Jan, and they knew that they were very near the end of their trail. Slocum's gun hand was itching. He wanted both of those men badly. He had almost forgotten about Jigs. But he wanted Sluice and Gillian. He could not remember ever wanting anyone in a worse way. Billy and Old Jan had most of the same reasons Slocum had, and Sheriff Holmes had his own reasons. But they all wanted the same thing. They all wanted it badly. They sat quietly around a small campfire sipping hot coffee. Soon, they would try to get some sleep. They would head on in to Devil's Gap with the first light of the morning.

At daylight, Sluice and Gillian woke up and got ready to ride back into town. First, they filled their pockets with gold coins once again. It was a short ride into Devil's Gap. The town had grown up in a hurry because of a recent gold strike. There were a few buildings thrown up with boards, but the town was mostly tents. There were businesses in tents, and people living in tents. Smoke was billowing up from just about every tent and building in the place. One long tent displayed a sign out front that read EATS. They stopped in front and tied their horses to an already crowded rail, and then went inside. Most of the tables were filled. The place was noisy. At last they spotted a table that was unoccupied. They headed for it and sat down. It was a few minutes before a man in a greasy apron came over to ask what they wanted.

"Coffee," said Sluice.

"And whatever you got for breakfast," Gillian said.

"Same thing for both of you?" the man asked.

"Same thing," said Gillian.

"Yeah," said Sluice.

The man went away, leaving Sluice and Gillian to sit and wait in the midst of all the talking and clattering of dishes. Sluice wanted to talk, but he couldn't think of anything to say, and besides, there was too much noise. They sat in silence waiting for their meals. At last, the man returned with their coffee. That was at least a relief. They sipped at the hot coffee, feeling it warm their guts. They had slurped their cups down about halfway when their breakfasts showed up. They each had a platter filled mostly with potatoes. There were two fried eggs on each and a slab of ham. Both men dug in and ate like it was their last meal. When they finished, they paid for the meals with a gold coin.

The man in the greasy apron looked astonished. He held up the coin in front of his face and stared at it. "I, uh, I got to make change for this," he said.

"Ain't you never seen real money before?" Gillian asked.

"Not around here," said the man. "Not very often."

He found the change he needed and gave it to Gillian. Then Gillian and Sluice walked out. They stood for a moment watching the people, almost all men, walk up and down the busy street, in and out of tent stores.

"Sluice," said Gillian, "there's opportunities in this town. I can see them."

"What are you thinking about?" Sluice said.

"Oh, maybe buying us a business. Maybe a gold mine. We'll have to nose around a bit first."

"Yeah," said Sluice. "Some kind of a business."

"Come on," said Gillian, and he led the way down the street. Now and then, he stopped to peer into a tent and see what was going on. He checked out each business as he passed by the tents. He saw money changing hands—well, mostly gold nuggets or gold dust.

"Yeah, Reb," said Sluice. "All kinds of opportunity around here."

A man came walking down the street toward them, and as he was about to pass them by, Gillian grabbed him by the arm.

"What the hell?" the man said.

"We're strangers in town," said Gillian. "Just got a question. That's all."

"Oh. Well, what is it?"

"We, me and my partner here, we're kind of interested in getting set up here with some kind of business. You know what I mean? Do you know of anything that's for sale?"

"Not much," the man said. "Most folks in town are doing so well right now they wouldn't sell out for nothing."

"Everyone's getting rich, huh?" said Sluice.

"Well, they're doing right good is what I'd say. But listen. Yeah. There's a miner up the hill yonder that just might sell out. He's getting old and tired. He just might sell out. Hell, he's got enough put away to last the rest of his life anyway."

"Can you point him out to us?" Gillian asked.

The man turned and pointed up the hillside. "You see that little shack up yonder, kind of nestled into the hillside?"

"Yeah," said Gillian.

"Well, that ain't no shack. Not really. That there's the entrance to his mine. The tent off to the right is where he lives. The only thing is, it won't be cheap."

"That's no problem to us," said Sluice.

"What's his name?" asked Gillian.

"Ezra Waits is what we call him," the man said.

"Thanks for the information," Gillian said.

"Sure thing," said the man as he walked on. Gillian stared at the mining shack and tent up on the hillside.

"You want to buy a mine?" said Sluice.

"We can pay someone to do all the work," Gillian answered. "We got plenty of cash."

"Yeah," Sluice said. "That's right. We could do that."

"With what we've already got," said Gillian, "and what comes out of that mine, we could be the richest sons of bitches for miles around. Hell, we could build our own opry house right here in Devil's Gap."

"Everyone would look up to us then," said Sluice.

"Damn right. Well, come on. Let's go."

"Where we going?"

"Up there to look at our mine," said Gillian.

Slocum, Holmes, Billy, and Old Jan rode into Devil's Gap around mid-morning. As they moved down the only street, they looked at all the faces in the bustling crowd. They did not recognize anyone. They rode clear to the opposite end of the street. Then they turned around and headed back again. They stopped in front of a large tent that had lettering painted on the front canvas: SALOON. They tied their horses at the rail and went inside. It was early in the day, but the place was already crowded. They stood near the bar and looked the crowd over. Still, they did not recognize anyone. Slocum was standing at Holmes's right.

"Are you sure they've got to be here?" he asked.

"There's no other place," said Holmes. "Not the direction they were headed. They're either out on the prairie or in town here."

"They're not out on the prairie," Slocum said.

Holmes shrugged. "Then they're here—somewhere."

A young girl appeared from out of the crowd and sidled up to Billy Pierce. Slocum thought that she looked more frightened than greedy. "Buy me a drink?" she said. Billy looked at Slocum.

"Go ahead," Slocum said.

Billy walked the girl to the bar and ordered a couple of drinks. Just then a big ugly man came out of the crowd. He spotted Billy and the girl. He stomped over to the bar and grabbed the girl by a shoulder, spinning her around.

"So here you are," he said.

"Leave me alone," she said.

"Come on, damn you," the man said.

"You heard the girl, mister," said Billy. "Leave her alone."

"She's with me," the man said. "You stay out of this."

"Mister, you—"

The man punched Billy in the jaw before Billy could finish what he was about to say, and Billy went sprawling on the floor. Slocum stepped up quickly.

"Hold on there," he said.

"Oh," said the big man. "You want her, too?"

20

"I just want you to back off," said Slocum. "Go on back over there and drink your whiskey."

"And I'm telling you to mind your own business, ass-hole," the man said, "if you don't want your head bashed in, too."

Slocum stomped the man's boot and felt bones crunch. The man yelled and grabbed his foot with both hands. While he was hopping on one foot, Slocum bashed him in the side of the head with a hard right. The man fell on the floor and lay still. Slocum reached down and pulled the six-gun from the man's waistband. He tossed it on the bar and said to the bartender, "Put that away." The barkeep took the gun and stashed it under the bar.

"You didn't have to do that, Slocum," said Billy.

"Ah, hell, I just felt like it," said Slocum.

"Thanks, mister," said the girl.

Billy ordered two drinks from the bartender, but when the drink was put in front of her, the girl took a tiny sip and coughed.

"You all right?" Billy asked.

"I didn't really want a drink," she said.

"But you—"

"I just wanted to get away from that—that man," she said,

and she looked with distaste at the man still lying unconscious on the floor. "And I don't want to be here when he wakes up."

"Well, where can you go?" said Billy.

"Come on," she said.

Billy looked at Slocum, and Slocum nodded. "Go on ahead with her," he said.

Billy let the girl lead him away. They went out of the tent saloon, and she led the way to a smaller tent and inside. There was a cot in there and not much else. She sat down on the cot and looked at the bare ground that served as a floor. Billy stared at her full of wonderment.

"Look," he said, "you don't have to— I mean, how long you been working in that place anyhow?"

"Just since this morning," she said. "That man—he was the first to—"

"He was the first one to try to get you—alone?"

"Yes."

"Well, how come you be in there in the first place?"

"My daddy was mining," she said. "Trying to anyway. He died a few days ago, and I run out of money pretty fast. I didn't seem to have no choice."

Billy looked at her for the first time. She was young, no more than twenty, he thought. She had long blond hair and big blue eyes. Her lips were full and red. The cheap outfit they had put her in showed off her ample shape. But she looked sweet and vulnerable. Billy suddenly felt responsible somehow.

"I don't want to go back in there," she said.

"You don't have to," said Billy.

"They'll come after me."

"Well, they'll have to get past me," he said. "And that won't be an easy thing."

"You mean that?"

"Of course I do. I don't say nothing I don't mean."

Back in the tent saloon, Holmes, Slocum, and Old Jan ordered a couple of drinks and sat down at a table. They kept watching the faces as new customers came into the place. Still, they recognized no one. Slocum started to say, "Holmes, are you sure—"

"They're here somewhere," the sheriff said. "I know it."

The big man on the floor stirred. He got himself to his feet and leaned on the bar. "Give me a whiskey," he said. The bartender poured him a drink, and the man paid for it. He drank it down. He felt for his six-gun and could not find it.

"Hey," he said, "where's my goddamn gun?"

The barkeep reached under the bar, pulled out the weapon, and tossed it on the bar in front of the man. The man picked it up, cocked it, and turned around looking. He spotted Slocum sitting at the table and pointed the gun in that direction.

"You son of a bitch," he roared.

Slocum's Colt was out and barking in no time at all. Two slugs tore into the man's chest, knocking him back against the bar. He sagged there for an instant, a stupid look on his already stupid-looking face. His fingers went limp, and he dropped the still-unfired gun to the floor. His elbows were on the bar holding him up. He slumped some more. His chin dropped to his chest. His elbows finally slipped off the bar, and he fell to the floor in a sitting position leaning back against the bar. He was dead.

In the small tent, Billy was sitting beside the girl. His arm was around her shoulders. She put her head on his chest. "What's your name?" he asked her.

"Maggie," she said. "Maggie Black."

"I'm Billy Pierce," he said. "I'm glad to meet you, Maggie."

She smiled for the first time. "I'm glad to meet you, Billy," she said. "Do you want to—"

"You don't have to do nothing," he said. "Besides, I wouldn't want to do it here. Not in this place."

She lifted her head and looked him in the face. "I like you," she said. "You're not like them others in the saloon. You're nice."

"Where's your stuff?" Billy asked her. "I mean, your clothes and all."

"I've still got Daddy's cabin," she said. "That's where I live. I don't have much, but all I've got is there."

"Well, let's go get it," Billy said. He took hold of the dress she was wearing. "We can give this thing back."

She smiled broadly. "All right," she said. "Come on."

Gillian and Sluice were at the mine on the side of the hill talking with the owner, Ezra Waits. The man on the street had been right. Old Waits wanted out. He was tired. He had pulled enough out of the mine to live well for the rest of his years, and he was more than willing to part with the mine. They agreed on a price, and the two outlaws had pulled all of the gold coins out of their pockets and laid them on Waits's table.

"That's a down payment," said Gillian. "We'll bring back the rest in about an hour. You have the papers ready by then."

"I sure will," said Waits.

"Where can we rent a wagon around here?" said Sluice.

"What you want with a wagon?" Waits asked.

"We mean to move right in," said Gillian. "We've got some supplies to haul up here."

"Hell," said the old man, "I've got a wagon right up here. You all can have it. It comes with the place."

They hitched up the wagon and drove down the hill, promising to return soon. The old man watched them drive down the hill, smiling at his good fortune. Once down the hill, Sluice and Gillian turned to drive down the only street in Devil's Gap. They moved past the tent saloon while Slocum, Holmes, and Old Jan still sat at the table drinking. They rolled on out to the shack they had commandeered at the edge of town. Soon, they had the gold loaded. They covered the bags the best they could, with weeds and sticks and even the logs from the old corral. Then they started back.

"You know, Sluice," Gillian said, "once we get them papers signed and all by that old fart, we could kill him."

"Then we'd have the mine and all our money back," said Sluice, a big grin on his face.

"Just my thoughts," said Gillian.

The man Sluice and Gillian had talked to on the street had a few friends gathered around him. They were lounging on the street talking and chewing, spitting on the street. The man said, "Say, boys, there was a couple of fellows here this morning asking about something they could buy around here. I told them about old Ezra's place, and they headed up there to check on it."

"Ezra might sell out?" said another.

"That's right," said the first man.

"Well, hell," said another. "Let's all go up there and see what's happened."

"Yeah. We can congratulate old Ezra and meet our new neighbors at the same time."

"If they made a deal," said the first man.

"Yeah. Well, maybe we'll find out."

They started walking, heading for the trail that would take them up the hillside.

Billy and Maggie arrived at the shack her father had left her, and went inside. Billy stood looking around for a moment. There wasn't much to see. It was just a basic place to live. There was a stove and a couple of cots. A table with two chairs stood in the center of the shack. It was neat and clean, though, as clean as such a place could be.

"Well," she said, "this is it. My home."

"It's better than the other place," said Billy.

"Do you have a home, Billy?" she asked.

"No," he said. "I guess I don't. I've just been a cowhand. Lived in the bunkhouses where I worked. That's all."

"You could live here with me," she said, and she walked up close to him and put her hands on his chest.

"Well, I—"

Her arms went around his shoulders, and she pulled his

face toward hers. Their lips met in a tender kiss. Then they parted again.

"I don't mind doing it with you," she said. "I want to."

Billy's heart pounded in his chest. He hugged her tight and kissed her again, this time longer and more passionately. She pulled him toward the cot and started pulling his shirt off over his head.

By the time Sluice and Gillian arrived back at Ezra Waits's mine, there was a gang gathered up there. The men were drinking and slapping Waits on the back, and they were all laughing and having a grand old time.

"Congratulations, Ezra," one of the men was saying. "By gum, I'd sure like to escape from this place the way you're doing."

"Damn right," said another man. "You've just managed what all of us would like to do."

"Say," said Waits, "here comes the new owners. Climb down, men, and meet some of your new neighbors."

Sluice and Gillian looked at one another and frowned. Gillian tied off the reins and climbed down out of the wagon. Sluice followed him. Waits made introductions all around, and Sluice and Gillian had to shake hands with all. They did their best to smile and act like they were pleased to meet everyone. They were offered some whiskey and, of course, they accepted. Soon, they were almost as drunk as all the others. Then Waits remembered something important.

"Say, fellows," he said, "did you bring the rest of my money?"

"Why, sure," said Gillian.

"I got these papers ready," Waits said. "I'll sign them over to you soon as you pay me off."

The other miners all watched with wide-open eyes as Gillian walked back to the wagon and dug through all the debris and into one of the bags. He came back with the cash, and the miners' eyes widened even more at the sight of real gold money. Waits signed the papers and handed them to Gillian.

"You're the proud owners of a good, working mine," he said.

"Yeah," said Gillian, still disappointed that there was a crowd around and he and Sluice could not go ahead with their murderous plan. One of the townsmen tipped back the last bottle of whiskey and emptied it. He held it up and shook it.

"Hey," he said, "we're all out of drink."

"Well, Goddamn it," said another. "We got to keep on celebrating old Ezra's good fortune."

"Let's all go down to the saloon," said Ezra. "I've done got my bag packed."

He ducked into the tent and dragged out a small bag.

"Is that all you've got?" Sluice asked.

"That's it," said Ezra. "The rest is all yours. Come on, boys. Let's get on down to the saloon." He turned to Sluice and Gillian. "You two coming along?"

"Uh, no, thanks," Gillian said. "I think we'll stay here and get settled in."

"Yeah," said Sluice. "We've got some things to take care of here."

The raucous crowd, including old Ezra, started on their way down the hill, singing and laughing all the way. Gillian and Sluice stood watching them go.

"Well," said Sluice, "there goes our money."

"Aw, hell," said Gillian, "we got plenty as it is. Maybe it's better this way. We don't need to start our new life in this town with a killing, now do we?"

"I guess you're right. Let's figure out where to hide our money away."

"Yeah," said Gillian.

The two started poking around in their new home.

Ezra and his pals reached the saloon and stormed in, making enough noise for a pack of buffalo hunters just hitting town after months out on the prairie. Everyone in the place turned to look at them. Ezra reached the bar first, and he pounded on it with his fist. The bartender walked over to him.

"Hey, Ezra," he said, "what the hell's wrong with you?"

"I want to buy drinks for everyone in the whole house," Ezra shouted.

"You sure about that?" said the barkeep.

"Hell, yes, I'm sure," Ezra said. "Start pouring."

"All right," said the barkeep. "Long as you know what you're doing." He turned and reached for the bottles, and started by pouring fresh drinks for everyone who was standing at the bar. Cheers and thanks to Ezra rang out around the room. When the bartender was through pouring drinks at the bar, he grabbed another couple of bottles and started making his way around to all the tables. He reached the table at which Slocum, Holmes, and Old Jan were seated, and he refilled their glasses.

"Say," said Holmes, "what do we owe this to?"

"Damned if I know," said the barkeep. "Old Ezra up there just come in and made an announcement that he wanted to buy everyone drinks. He ain't never been this crazy before. He's been making a living up at his place, but maybe he just struck the mother lode. Who knows?"

When the bartender went back behind the bar, Ezra pulled some coins out of his pocket and tossed them on the counter. The ring of the gold coins could be heard over the general noise in the saloon. In case someone had not heard, a voice at the bar said, "Goddamn, Ezra. Where the hell did you get all them gold coins?"

"I just sold my claim is what," Ezra answered.

Holmes stood up and walked to the bar. He got there just before the barkeep swept the coins up.

"Wait a minute," he said. "Can I have a look at that?"

"Why not?" said the barkeep. He passed one coin to Holmes. "We don't see much real cash around here."

Holmes looked at the coin and handed it back. He turned to Ezra and said, "You got that from selling your claim?"

"That's right," said Ezra.

"Who'd you sell it to?"

"Couple of strangers," said Ezra, "names of Gillian and Godfrey."

"Reb Gillian and Sluice Godfrey?" said Holmes.

"Yeah," said Ezra. "That's them. Friends of yours?"

21

Gillian and Sluice stashed all their stolen gold inside the mine entrance. When they were finished, they sat down to rest. Neither one cared for hard work. "We got any whiskey?" Sluice asked.

"No. Let's go into town for some," said Gillian.

They got up and went to their horses. Mounting up, they headed down the hill.

In the neighboring shack just to the north, Billy Pierce and Maggie were naked in bed. Billy had been hesitant because of Maggie's circumstances and what she had just been through, but when he saw that she was more than willing, he joined in with just as much glee. Maggie was on the cot first, and Billy crawled on top of her, careful not to hurt her. She was precious to him. Keeping his weight on his hands and knees, he leaned forward to kiss her. With their lips pressing together, she wrapped her arms around his neck and pulled him downward. Breaking away from the kiss, she said, "It's all right, Billy. Lay on me. I want to feel your weight on me."

Billy eased himself down on her smooth body. He felt the touch of her from his head to his toes, and it thrilled him more than anything else in his young life ever had. But he was afraid to do anything to her. He did not want to seem to be overanxious, and he did not want to hurt her. She sensed his hesitation, and she pulled his face down to hers again and kissed him again, this time deeply. While they were thus engaged, she reached down between their bodies with both hands and found his young and throbbing tool. She grasped it hard, and Billy gasped out loud.

Maggie guided the anxious rod into her soft, wet slit and thrust her hips upward, sucking the entire length into her. "Oh," said Billy. "Oh. Oh." He began to respond to her movements, and soon they were moving in unison, like a well-oiled machine. He humped and thrust with all his might, and suddenly he felt himself begin to gush forth, over and over. At last, he was spent. He lay on her heavily, gasping for breath. She hugged him tight and kissed him over and again.

"In a little while," she said, "we can do it another time."

It took some doing, but Slocum and Holmes managed to get Ezra outside the saloon and made him point out the place he had sold to Gillian and Sluice. When he had done that, he broke loose and went back inside. Slocum, Holmes, and Old Jan stood staring up at the mine entrance and the tent. "He said he left them up there," said Holmes.

"Yeah," said Slocum.

"You want to go up there after them?" said Holmes.

"If they're still up there," said Old Jan, "we'd be easy targets on that trail."

"He's right, Slocum," said Holmes.

Slocum knew they were right, but he was itching to kill. It had been a long road, and he was anxious to have it all over with. Both men needed to be killed.

"Let's sit right here," he said, "and watch that trail."

They dragged three chairs out of the saloon and sat down outside just to the right of the entrance. All three stared at the trail up the side of the hill.

Jigs and his bunch came riding into Devil's Gap. The street was crowded as usual, and Slocum and the other two men did not see them coming. "Say, there's a saloon up yonder," said Bo. "Let's hit it." They angled their horses toward the big tent, working their way through the mess of foot, horseback, and wagon traffic. When they finally broke through, Jigs recognized the three men sitting outside the saloon. Jigs nearly fell off his horse in panic, but he jerked out his six-gun and fired a shot that just missed Slocum and went through the canvas wall of the tent saloon. Someone inside yelped.

Slocum threw himself from the chair onto the ground and pulled out his Colt at the same time. His shot had to be true. There were too many people around. He fired, and the bullet ranged upward, hitting Jigs under the chin and coming out the back of his head. He was dead in the saddle. His head bobbled foolishly on his shoulders for a moment before he toppled to the street.

At the same time, Holmes and Old Jan had drawn their revolvers and jumped up from their chairs, moving to the sides. They were looking for a way to shoot without endangering innocent people. Bo, Limpy, and Bernie had all hauled out their own weapons, but Limpy and Bernie had turned their horses and were trying to make a getaway through the crowd. Bo was trying to aim his revolver, but his horse would not be still. Holmes moved out in the street and grabbed hold of Bo's shirt, pulling him out of the saddle. Bo landed hard on the ground, dropping his gun. Holmes pounded Bo's face with his fists.

Slocum fought his way through the crowd to jump on the back of Limpy's horse. His right arm encircled Limpy's neck. His left grabbed Limpy's gun hand. He wrestled with Limpy until they both fell from the saddle. Bernie had made his way through the crowd to the other side of the street, and was trying to get back out of town the way he had come in. Old Jan grabbed a rifle from a man standing nearby and squeezed his way through the crowd. Bernie was riding away. Old Jan leveled the rifle and fired, and Bernie toppled out of the saddle. The crowd was going wild. Old Jan returned the rifle to its owner. Working his way back through the crowd, he helped Slocum drag Limpy to his feet and shove him back toward the tent saloon. Holmes already had a bloody Bo huddled up there.

"We should've killed them," Slocum said. "You said there ain't no jail here."

"We'll tie them tight and hold them till I'm ready to ride out of here," Holmes said. "I'll take them back to my jail."

Billy had discovered that Maggie had no food in her shack. He still had a little money in his jeans, and so he volunteered to go back down into town and buy some groceries. He had heard the shooting, but from up on the hill, he could not see what was happening. Finally, the shooting had stopped. The traffic seemed to be moving normally along the street, so he told Maggie to wait for him there, and he headed on down on horseback. In a few minutes, he was part of the crowd. He rode past the saloon and saw his partners. He stopped and dismounted.

"Well, Billy," said Old Jan, "you been having yourself a time, have you?"

"Jan," said Billy, "she ain't what you think. She's a good girl. I'm fixing to marry up with her."

"You're what?" said Slocum.

Billy told the story of what had happened to Maggie's father and how Maggie, desperate, had gone to work in the saloon.

"That man you hit in the saloon," he said to Slocum, "he was the first one that got after her."

"Oh," Slocum said. "So she's got a place here?"

"Yeah," said Billy. "Right up yonder." He pointed to a small shack that was next in line to the one Sluice and Gillian had just purchased. "It was her dad's place, but he died before he could really get started working it. She didn't know what to do. I told her I'd work it for her. Well, for us."

"So you mean to settle down here?" said Old Jan.

Billy looked down at his boots. "Well, yeah," he said. "I reckon. I mean, well, hell, I'm still with you guys. Till we get the job done. I ain't running out on you or nothing like that."

"Billy," said Slocum, "we've got Sheriff Holmes here with us now. You don't have to follow this thing through. We'll get it done all right."

"No," Billy said. "I'm with you. I been with you all this way, and I'm in it till the end."

"All right," Slocum said. "It's up to you. You ought to know, though, that Sluice and Gillian are right up there." He pointed. "The place right next to yours."

"They up there now?" Billy asked.

"Far as we know," Slocum said.

"We just met the old man who sold it to them," said Old Jan. "He's in the bar spending those gold coins they stole."

"I'll be damned," said Billy. "Well, what are you planning to do?"

"We're going to watch that path that goes up there," Slocum said. "Try to catch them on their way down into town. We don't want to fight them down here."

"Too many people," said Holmes.

"Yeah," said Old Jan. "We had one fight down here already."

"That was you?" said Billy. "I heard the shots. What happened?"

"Remember Jigs and Limpy and them?" Old Jan said.

"Yeah. Sure."

"They came riding in just as big as you please. Saw us before we saw them and started shooting. We didn't have a choice. Slocum killed Jigs. I shot one of them others. I don't know his name. We got the last two all hog-tied. Holmes is going to take them to his jail when he goes."

"Well, I'll be damned. I thought that Limpy and them other two was going to Texas," Billy said.

"They should have," said Slocum.

"I'll be damned. And I missed the whole thing."

"You didn't miss much, pard," Slocum said.

"You don't need me just now, do you?" Billy asked. "I come back down here to get some groceries for Maggie. She ain't got no food up at her place."

"Then I'd say go get the groceries," Slocum said. "Nothing more's going to happen down here for a spell."

"You sure?"

"Go on."

Billy mounted his horse and rejoined the heavy traffic moving down the street. He was soon out of sight. Old Jan, still watching the path up the hill, said, "Slocum. Look."

Slocum looked up the path and saw the figures of Sluice and Gillian on horseback coming down toward town.

"Let's go," he said. They rushed to their horses and mounted up. Fighting their way through the crowd, they reached the bottom of the path and headed up. Each man had his rifle out and ready. They made it about a quarter of the way up. Gillian and Sluice were about halfway down. The two killers pulled their rifles loose, put the rifles to their shoulders, and fired quick shots. The bullets came close, but not close enough. Slocum returned fire. His shot knocked the hat off Sluice's head.

"Goddamn," Sluice shouted.

Holmes fired and hit Gillian in the thigh.

"Ah," Gillian shouted. "The son of a bitch got me."

Old Jan fired and missed. Each of the three men cranked shells into the chambers of their rifles as Gillian and Sluice turned their horses and headed back for their mining camp.

"Come on," said Slocum. "We can't let them get set up there."

They kicked their horses into a run, hurrying after their prey. If Sluice and Gillian got themselves under cover too fast, Slocum and his partners would still be out in the open on the path. They were closing the gap fast. Sluice dismounted first. He did not wait for Gillian. He ran for cover toward the mine entrance. Gillian kicked his horse in the sides and headed for an outcropping of rocks nestled against the hillside. He dropped out of the saddle and limped behind the rocks.

Slocum was the first of his bunch to reach the camp. He vaulted from the saddle and ducked into the tent with his

Winchester. He cranked a shot into the chamber and looked out toward the mine entrance and then the outcropping. He knew where Holmes and Old Jan were hidden, but he could not see either one. Holmes had ducked behind an old ore car that was sitting unused outside the entrance to the mine, and Old Jan had dropped down behind a wooden barrel. They waited. The atmosphere was thick with tension.

At last, Slocum fired at the outcropping. His shot hit the boulder that Gillian was behind. Old Jan and Holmes fired just after. Their shots also hit the boulder. Far from smoking Gillian out, the shots just made him duck deeper down behind his cover. There was no sign of any resistance yet coming from either Sluice or Gillian.

Down the hill, Billy Pierce was returning to Maggie's shack with a load of groceries. He heard the shots first. Then he saw Old Jan and Holmes, and he knew that Slocum was up there somewhere. He considered going up to join them, but then he changed his mind. He reached the place where the path forked and the trail he would follow to Maggie's place diverged from the main path. He followed that one, heading on back to Maggie's. Along the way, he heard a couple more shots. When he reached Maggie's shack, he found her standing outside. He dismounted, pulling his rifle out of the saddle boot.

"Get back inside, Maggie," he said.

"What is it?" she asked.

"Just get in the house," he said.

Maggie did as she was told, and Billy hurried over to a boulder up against the hillside. From there, he had a view of the neighboring mine, and he saw Gillian behind his boulder. He took a careful aim with his rifle and pulled the trigger. Gillian jerked and yelled. As he did, he moved and exposed himself, and Old Jan and Holmes both fired, knocking him down. He lay still. It was deathly quiet again.

Slocum stared at the mine entrance there before him. He knew that Sluice was in there. This was the end of his long trail. One way or the other, it would be finished here and now. He put the Winchester down on the cot inside the tent and pulled out his Colt. He cocked it. Sluice could be standing ready just inside the entrance, just inside the door to the half-shack that was built against the hill. If Slocum should expose himself, Sluice might have a good shot. Slocum thought for a moment. Then he called out to Old Jan and Holmes.

"Pepper that mine entrance," he said.

Both men started shooting. It sounded like a small war. Splinters flew from the wooden framework that covered the entrance to the mine. If Sluice was standing there near the doorway, he would have backed up to escape that barrage. Slocum came suddenly out of the tent and ran toward the entrance. The barrage let up as he was about to come into the path of the bullets. Reaching the doorway, he threw himself inside and on the ground, rolling over as he landed. He looked around. Sluice was not in sight. Slocum stood up, still searching the semidarkness there. He cocked his Colt again. Sluice had gone deeper into the mine. There was no other possibility.

Slocum started moving cautiously into the mine. His eyes slowly adjusted to the darkness. Up ahead was a turn in the mine shaft, and as Slocum approached it, Sluice suddenly jumped out and started firing his six-gun. A bullet nicked Slocum's left shoulder. Slocum fired one round. Sluice jerked and twitched as the bullet smashed his sternum. He tried to lift his gun to fire again. Slocum sent another shot into his chest, and Sluice fell over onto his back.

Slocum walked over to check, and found that Sluice was dead. He heaved a heavy sigh of relief and holstered his six-gun. Then, taking hold of one ankle of the corpse so he could drag it behind him, he started walking back toward the entrance to the mine.

When the shooting stopped, Billy and Maggie made their way over to the neighboring mine. The bodies of the two outlaws were thrown side by side, and the living started to search the whole area. They soon found the bags of gold. It was most of what Gillian and his gang had stolen.

"I don't think anyone will worry about what little is

missing," Holmes said. "They'll just be damn glad to get this much back. I think I'll just commandeer that wagon over there and load it up with this gold and my two prisoners down there and head for home."

"We'll help you get started," Slocum said. Before long, the sheriff was on his way. The others stood and watched him go for a couple of minutes. Then Billy Pierce spoke up.

"Say, I did bring home the groceries," he said. "How about we all go over to Maggie's place—"

"Our place," Maggie corrected.

Billy grinned and ducked his head. "Yeah," he said. "Our place, and have us a good meal."

Slocum looked at Old Jan. "That sounds like a fine idea," he said.

"So you're going to stay here and work a mine?" Old Jan asked Billy.

"Yeah," said Billy. "I think I will."

"What do you know about mining anyhow?"

"Not much," Billy admitted.

"Well, then," said Old Jan, "in that case, if you two don't mind, I just might hang around here with you and help you get started."

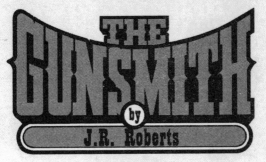